Hank

Hank

JAMES SAUER

Fic
SAU

Delacorte Press

Published by
Delacorte Press
Bantam Doubleday Dell Publishing Group, Inc.
666 Fifth Avenue
New York, New York 10103

Library of Congress Cataloging in Publication Data

Sauer, James.
    Hank / by James Sauer.
    p.   cm.
    Summary: Richard learns some lessons about
life and relationships with the opposite sex from
his younger brother Hank.
    ISBN 0–385–30034–4
    [1. Brothers—Fiction. 2. Family life—Fiction.]
I. Title.
    PZ7.S2499Han   1990
    [Fic]—dc20   89–23276
                                                      CIP
                                                      AC

Book design by Robin Arzt

Manufactured in the United States of America

April 1990

10   9   8   7   6   5   4   3   2   1

BVG

For Karen

Hank

CHAPTER 1

 My mom's an evening supervisor in the women's department at a store called Gilbert's. She's waiting for a day position to open up, but the woman she'd replace is totally committed to cosmetics. Even if that gal did shock the fashion world by quitting, I don't think the store would switch Mom to days, because there's a lot of shoplifting in the evening, and Mom's good at spotting the ladies that are coming out of the changing room wearing four dresses underneath their coats. When she catches somebody, Mom can get them to admit what they're up to without calling mall security right away, which the store appreciates. Even though most shoplifters

aren't armed, you don't want the ones who are, getting spooked.

The store also appreciates the way Mom keeps the high school girls who work the evening shift from squirting themselves with cologne ten times an hour. She's never a jerk about it, and some of the girls at my high school think Mom's great, but that's because she's never come into their rooms at dawn.

"Son?" she said after half opening my door the first day of my junior year.

"I'm sleeping in here, Mom."

"May I come in?"

"No."

"I'd like to talk to you."

"I'm in my underwear."

"What about the pajamas we gave you for Christmas?"

"What about them?"

"Don't you wear them?"

"I thought they were a gag gift."

"Could you cover up, please?"

"Why?"

"So I can come in."

"Don't guys usually get more privacy as they get older?" I asked while I pulled the sheet up.

"Generally speaking, yes."

"I don't think it's a general thing at all," I said, but Mom came into the room anyway.

"We have to talk before your father wakes up."

"Are you going to ask me again to go out to the backyard for some early morning thing?"

"No."

"This isn't about me going outside with you to see how the sun hits our apple tree at dawn?"

"This is about you taking the garbage out to the alley before your dad sees it."

"He's the one who told me to get rid of it. I think he figured last night that the house was starting to fill up with radon gas."

"Did he want the trash bags put on the porch?"

"He didn't say."

"I don't think he expected you to put garbage where I'd have to climb over it when I came home from work."

"Then he should've taken it out himself."

"Didn't we agree it was to be your responsibility?"

"Generally speaking, yes."

Mom smiled at my copying what she'd said a minute before, but she didn't make any room-leaving moves, and I knew the only way to get rid of her would be to agree that Dad gets weird whenever he does the garbage.

It isn't actually the trash that makes him crazy as much as it is the way the lane that runs through the middle of the block gets junked up. Every house used to have garbage cans that dogs scrounged around in, and whenever Dad found a hound with its head stuck in our trash, he'd whack the side of the can hard enough that a week later the dog's eyes would still be pinballing.

You'd think something like that would've cut down on the scrounging, but it didn't and the city finally filled the alleys with giant rubber tubs that looked like above-ground sewage tanks. Even if the dogs could've gotten up into them, I don't think they would've wanted to, but that didn't make Dad happy because the lids were impossible to raise if you had garbage in your arms, and most of the people in the neighborhood propped the tops open with sticks. The trash that blew out of the open tubs made Dad crazy, and he was going to install handles on all the lids until Mom found out and made him promise to let me take the garbage out from then on.

That worked until I stored the trash overnight on the porch. And when I wouldn't get up the next morning, Mom opened the shades I'd installed when my brother Hank had moved out of the room we'd been sharing. Hank used to get his bed lined up so the sun'd wake him when it rose, which I hated because even if I slept with my head in a closet, a belt buckle or something else you'd never think of would angle a reflection into my eyes. Hank was sorry whenever that happened, but it never made him leave the curtains closed.

When I told Dad about the reflection, he just asked if I knew it took a particle of light eight minutes to travel from the sun to Earth.

And when I told Mom I was going to go blind if Hank didn't get his own bedroom, she said, "Hank's very fond of you."

"He could be fond of me from across the hallway."

"He likes to talk with you while he falls asleep."

"He just wants to tell me what he did all day, and it's usually stupid stuff like how he watched plumbers hook up pipes in a new house."

"Do they still use solder that has to be heated on little burners?"

"What?"

"What kind of solder do plumbers use now?"

"How should I know?"

"I thought Hank might've mentioned it."

"If he did, I didn't listen."

"Do you ever tell him about your day?"

"What difference does it make what I tell him? The problem is how he gets up in the middle of the night and opens the curtains no matter how many times I ask him not to."

"Have you talked to your father about it?"

"He thinks I should be grateful the sun gets here as fast as it does."

"In another year your brother will be in school, and he'll want his own room."

"I'm stuck until then?"

"If you're willing."

"Can I at least tie him up before I go to sleep?"

"I think it'd hurt his feelings." Which I already knew, because Hank's an emotional kid. Last summer he was in love, which you wouldn't expect a nine-year-old kid to be except with his family and, if he's goofy like Hank, maybe with somebody like the unemployed guys who pick up cans in the alley—Hank saved his cans in the closet next to the refrigerator, and when he'd hear somebody going through the garbage, he'd grab the sack he had the cans in and run out the back door. He never talked to the alley guys, and I asked him once why he bothered with anybody who dug around in trash.

"They're okay," Hank said. "Picking up cans is just their job."

"Then why not throw your cans away like everybody else?"

"I don't think they like going through our garbage."

"You think everybody should take their cans out the way you do?"

"That'd be nicer."

"That'd be crazy," I said.

"We don't throw our letters away and make the mailmen look for them."

"It's not the same."

"Why not?"

"Because the guys in the alley aren't mailmen."

"So?"

"So digging around through garbage is probably more a hobby with them than a job."

"I don't think so," Hank said.

"Do they ever thank you?"

"No."

"Don't you think they'd thank you if they appreciated it?"

"Maybe they can't. Maybe they're all speechless."

"You mean mutes?"

"That's probably why they don't have regular jobs and have to go up and down the alley looking for cans."

That was Hank when he was nine, and you can see how he'd fall in love earlier than most kids. Not that there's anything wrong with falling in love. But even Hank must've known nine's pretty young, because whenever I'd tease him about Emily, he'd act like I didn't know what I was talking about. And maybe I didn't. But last summer, after Emily's family'd moved into the neighborhood, Hank hung around our front porch a lot more than usual, and he was always there to watch whenever Emily'd walk by wearing a hat that flopped down over her face and old-fashioned dresses that reached all the way down to the sidewalk.

Usually when a kid dresses for the wrong century, she belongs to a family where everybody wears crazy clothes, so I expected Emily to walk by sometime with a bunch of brothers and sisters who looked like circus clowns. But Emily turned out to have only one sister and no brothers, and the sister didn't wear stuff that you'd see in a museum the way Emily did.

A guy who knew the family pointed Emily's sister out to me once at the swimming pool. He said her name was Allie Boggs and would've introduced me but I wasn't interested. Emily's sister looked okay in a swim suit, but the guy mentioned how she was a year younger than me, and I'm not interested in fifteen-year-olds, especially if they've still got braces on their teeth the way the Boggs girl did. I'm not a snob or anything; it's just that younger girls either won't shut up or they're as silent as the guys Hank gives aluminum to. What I go for are seniors, though usually they don't go for me. My sister's a senior, and she says older girls aren't interested in me because I'm a jerk, though I think Liz is just embarrassed that I'm always trying to date up her friends—my sister's real name is Elizabeth, and lately that's what she wants everybody to call her, but I don't because she's such a pain.

At the end of last summer Liz made a big deal about how she couldn't wait for school to start—like she was so adult, she saw it as an opportunity. Hank was just as bad, except he wanted school to get going so he could hang around Emily.

It would've taken a hundred teen models transferring to my school to get me excited about the coming year, and I don't know if even that would've done it, because I go to a private school where they never let the girls do too much advertising with what they wear. I don't mean we have to dress in uniforms, because the school's not that exclusive; in fact, they'll take just about anybody, and you don't have to be rich or Catholic to get in, though that's pretty much who goes there.

I think parents have the idea that because the campus has a lot of lawns their kids will get in less trouble than if they were hanging around on pavement. I don't know why else anyone'd send their kids there, especially for twelve years, which is how long I'm going to end up putting in.

There's different buildings for the grade school and high school, but we all ride the same buses, and the first day of school Hank sat in his bus seat staring like mad at Emily. He hadn't talked to her yet, and I don't think he could believe how lucky he was that she was going to his school. Even so, he should've been more subtle because she might've noticed how he was eyeballing her and punched him. If you think a nine-year-old girl wouldn't be up to that, you're wrong. There was this kid who kept making jokes about Emily's antique clothing; and instead of saying something back or ignoring the kid, Emily took a long pin out of the brim of her hat and stabbed at the kid's hand. The pin went into the space between two of the kid's fingers and got buried so deep in the seat, Emily had trouble pulling it out. The kid who'd been making jokes must've thought his hand was stuck, because while Emily was trying to get her weapon back, the kid sat there and screamed until the bus driver pulled over. When the driver came back and saw what was going on, he gave Emily a lecture about how riding the bus was a privilege which anybody who went around spearing people wasn't going to keep for very long.

I thought my brother'd get discouraged, seeing how dangerous Emily was, but he didn't, and actually she wasn't the most dangerous one on the bus. There was a guy named Stratton who was worse. Last year Stratton pulled the pants off a freshman as a joke or something; and instead of walking up the aisle in his underwear to let the driver know what'd happened, the kid begged Stratton to give the pants back. Stratton teased the kid for a little while and then tossed the clothes out a window.

The kid would've had to get off the bus in his underwear if my brother hadn't just been dropped off and seen the clothes fly out the bus window. Hank ran the pants up to the high school drop-off, and when he came on the bus, he was pretty loud asking whose clothes he had. The freshman claimed the pants without saying thanks, which I can understand because one time I was hanging around the living room trying to impress a couple of my sister's friends when Hank walked in and told me that the cows were getting out of the barn. We're not farmers or anything, so I didn't get what Hank was talking about until he pointed at my zipper. I looked to see how seriously down the zipper was, and it was half-way. I pulled it up and thought about explaining that I was having a lot of trouble lately with defective zippers, but I figured nobody'd believe a lie like that so I didn't bother.

I wanted to clobber Hank for embarrassing me, but I didn't, because he never got why you were mad. I mean, when he did something stupid, he didn't mind everyone laughing about it—not that he went around doing stuff wrong just to entertain people. In fact, for a kid he did a lot of stuff right. But when he did blow it, it was just as funny to him as it was to everybody else. So he wouldn't have understood why that kid on the bus was too embarrassed to say anything. Not that getting thanked was why Hank did stuff. He'd do something for you even if he didn't like you.

Hank had this idea that everything had a way it was supposed to be. A right way that wasn't easy or maybe even appreciated, but that was right just the same. Like this '36 Plymouth an old guy across the street owned, which according to Hank looked the way a car should look. I don't know what made my brother an expert on car design, but he said the builder of that car had gotten it right, and that just about everybody since had gotten it wrong.

Most of the time when he talked about that stuff, I ignored him. But once, during a sophomore football game when I'd been banged up and was lying on the sidelines, Hank climbed over the fence that's around the field and said, "You got it right."

"Do I have to get killed to get it right?" I asked him.

"Sometimes."

"Then I'd rather get it wrong," I said, and Hank was going to say something back, but a coach came along and ran my brother off.

I laid around after that and watched a linebacker for the other team chase our quarterback across the field. Everybody on the sidelines was yelling for the quarterback to throw the ball, but I was hoping the linebacker'd catch him and break his arm. I know that's the sort of thing you're not supposed to think when you're on a ball club, but I can't stand all that spirit stuff. I mean, nobody we played against could've been suiting up as many jerks as our team was. Our quarterback, for example, expected you to get open deep on every pass play, but when you finally did, he'd be in the backfield wondering if his helmet was flattening his hair.

On the play where I'd gotten hurt, he threw a rainbow that I had to slide along the ground to slow up for, and I was in the middle of making a spectacular over-the-shoulder catch when the other team's secondary caught up to me.

If you get trampled the way I did, you can't catch anything. But even poked full of holes the way I was, I felt pretty good about how I'd tried to make the play. I didn't tell that to Hank, though, because he's nuts enough about that getting-it-right business without me encouraging him.

CHAPTER 2

That guy Stratton I told you about had a girlfriend who rides our bus, and the first day of school I thought I saw her giving me the eye; so when the bus stopped, I went over and sat next to her. I said hello but she just turned away, and she didn't look at me even when she explained how she was going to scratch out my eyes if I kept on talking to her. I figured I'd been wrong about her being interested in me and would've gone back to my seat except the driver won't let you walk around while the bus is moving. That was okay with me, because we were still a mile from where we'd picked up Stratton the year before. I didn't know that his family had moved.

When the bus stopped again, Stratton got on before I could get up. You could tell he was upset about me being next to his girlfriend, and what I should've done was jump out a window, but I got so paralyzed by fear that Stratton had to pick me up and carry me to the back of the bus. After he'd shoved me into an empty seat, he gave my neck a chop that was too small for the bus driver to see but big enough to cave in the front of my neck. With my throat collapsed, breathing got to be pretty tricky, and I was trying to get some air into my lungs when my brother and sister showed up. Hank sat down next to me and watched while Liz felt my neck like she was a doctor, which as far as I knew she wasn't.

I tried to tell her to knock it off, but all I could get out of my mouth were barking sounds; and when I went to shove Liz away, she slapped my hands and told me I'd gotten what I deserved for bothering a senior girl. I would've given her a chop in the throat except I noticed she'd brought along her clarinet case. I started wondering why she was packing her instrument, but before my voice came back enough to ask, the bus stopped to pick up more kids, and Liz went over to Stratton. You could tell he didn't like whatever Liz was telling him, but when he started to get out of his seat, she swung her clarinet case into his chest. He turned white like his summer tan had been recalled and sat back down.

His girlfriend got up and made some threats, but

Liz ignored her and walked back up to the front of the bus.

When my breathing got going again Hank said, "He's a lot bigger than you," meaning Stratton. I didn't want to get into a conversation right then, because Hank would've wanted to talk about how I should've gone over and demanded an apology or done something else that would've meant another throat-chop, so I ignored him. When we reached Hank's school, I didn't say good-bye because I was mad he had all these expectations I wasn't living up to, and I wanted him to know I was sore, which I'm sure he did because he's a sensitive kid. Too sensitive.

CHAPTER 3

I hope you weren't surprised when Liz said that thing on the bus about me getting what I deserved, because we didn't get along like when we were kids. Liz used to show me stuff like how if a mosquito is biting you, you can squeeze around the sticker so that the bug keeps filling up with blood until it pops. Maybe that sounds gross, but when you're a kid it's neat.

Actually, I still think it's interesting, but Liz sure doesn't. Once recently she had friends over for pizza, and just for something to talk about I explained that mosquito thing. Liz didn't talk to me for a week after that, which was no great loss. Not like it would've been when we were kids and catching bees so we could start our own hive.

That was an idea I'd had, and if at the time Liz thought it was stupid, she didn't say anything. In fact, no matter how dumb I got, Liz wouldn't tell me what to do unless I asked. Even when I put a bagful of captured bees into my pocket, Liz didn't give me a speech about how dumb I was being.

When the bees tried to sting their way out, I ran around the yard yelling like crazy, and Liz had to tackle me to get the bag out of my pocket.

Later, when I was telling Dad how every bee had stung me and Liz a dozen times, he said that bees die after stinging once. I guess that was supposed to make me feel sorry for them, but it didn't.

After Liz'd gotten the bag out of my pocket, she hauled me over to the garden hose, and while I slid my pants off, she mixed up some mud that she spread on my leg. Then, one by one, Liz took the stingers out. She didn't get around to taking care of her hand until she was done with me, and if you had to have a sister when you were a kid, Liz was the best you could get.

Hank still got along with her, but that's no big deal, because he got along with everybody—Dad says Hank's like Liz when she was younger. He says they both had the same sense of wonder, which is just the sort of screwball thing Dad would say. He analyzes everything, and it doesn't matter what it is you're talking about. The day Liz showed me how to blow up mosquitoes, I came home and was telling Dad about it, but he interrupted and said, "She."

"What?"

"You keep calling the mosquitoes he or him, Son, but only the female bites. She needs the blood to nourish the eggs she's carrying."

Dad comes up with sick stuff like that all the time. Once when I tried to explain what a pain Liz'd become, he said that kids are like caterpillars who need watching so they don't get run over in the driveway before they turn into the butterflies children are secretly becoming.

The only part of that whole thing which made any sense was how Liz'd been looking buglike since middle school. Lately she'd lightened up on the makeup, but she was still camping out in the bathroom every morning so she could weird out her hair. When she was a kid she used to wear it pulled back in a ponytail, which I thought looked great, but last summer she started going out with a guy named Matt, whose family is loaded. The guy's dad is president of a slaughterhouse in Billings, and you'd think a family like that'd always be talking about the price of pork bellies, but the women in Matt's family are the type who get their pores sewn shut because they figure sweating is low class. In fact, if Liz goes to school without looking like she's on her way to interview for a modeling job, Matt's two sisters will come over at lunch and make a big deal about how they'd never have the courage to ignore fashion trends the way Liz does. Actually, that's a weird thing for them to say, because most of the time Liz wears sharp outfits, and I don't think she'd mind what those snobs thought except they always show up when Matt and Liz are together. Usually Matt tells them that they're an embarrassment to him or something else that gets him in trouble with his mother.

Anymore Liz just tries to avoid giving those gals the chance to hassle her, which means she's in the bathroom so long in the morning that I'm lucky to get ten seconds in there after she's done.

I told Dad we had to add another bathroom to our house, but he just said that my great-grandfather lived his entire life on a farm that didn't have indoor plumbing. When I mentioned how I didn't see what that had to do with anything, Dad gave me a speech about how spoiled kids are today, and I started worrying that instead of adding a bathroom on, he'd tear the one we already had out.

I don't really have that much to do in the john in the morning anyway, and Liz's hogging the place wouldn't have bothered me except she always locked herself in. I suppose there's a lot of people who do that, but with Liz it was because I'd barged in on her once. It was no big incident, because the door'd been open a little, and I knew she was just painting her face. But when I told her it was too early to get ready for Halloween, she tried to stuff a tube of lipstick up my nose. That's the sort of thing which can hurt, but what bothered me more was seeing that Liz didn't care about my opinion anymore.

After that I started giving her a hard time whenever I could, which's one of the reasons I kept asking her friends out. So it wasn't a big shock to me that she wasn't sympathetic on the bus after Stratton'd clobbered me.

CHAPTER 4

When the bus ride ended that first day of school, I got away from everyone as fast as I could, and that included Emily's sister, Allie.

If you didn't figure out that she was riding, that's okay, because half the people on the bus didn't notice her either. Mostly she stared out the window, except when Emily tried to stab that kid's hand. Then Allie went back to help the bus driver, and it looked like she'd had plenty of practice taking dangerous stuff away from her sister.

Emily was wearing one of those antique dresses I'd seen her in all summer; but instead of the sneakers she usually tramped around in, she was wearing black shoes that came up over her ankles. They were pretty weird looking and would've taken a year to lace up, except instead of laces there were snaps and buckles that you probably had to go to a special school to learn how to operate.

If it sounds like I was spending a lot of time watching Allie and Emily, I wasn't. It's just that I like to study little things people do—Dad says that if you pay attention, you'll know more about people twenty minutes after meeting them than they find out about themselves in a lifetime; like when I saw Allie looking out the bus window most of the route, I figured she was shy, but later when I saw her walking in the halls, I knew I'd been wrong, because she didn't walk like someone who's shy. I won't bore you with how one walk's different from another, because if I know so much, how did I let myself get stuck with Mr. Fielding for homeroom?

He's an okay guy, I guess, and one time he saw me at the supermarket and remembered my name, which is unusual for a teacher at my school. But the first day of homeroom he handed out three pages of rules and started reading them to us. Homeroom's only five minutes long and at the bell Fielding told us to hold on to the rules, but almost everybody went from homeroom to math, and I don't think one copy made it through that first hour class.

Math pretty much puts me to sleep, and I haven't even got a checkbook, because balancing it would be such a bore. Not that I have much money to worry about, because most of the jobs high school kids get pay slave wages. I more or less depend on my parents to keep me out of poverty, though I did get a job last summer riding a lawn mower around a city park, which paid pretty good. But the work was boring and I kept napping off. When that happened, I usually ran into a tree or a swing set or something else that'd get me stopped without any damage being done. But one time I drove over a blanket two people were picnicking on. I didn't mow them up or anything, but they got upset anyway and tried to get me fired. My boss is an okay guy, and when the couple was done telling him what'd happened and had taken off, my boss laughed and made me tell him a couple times how I'd woken up and seen plastic silverware shooting out from underneath the mower and the couple diving for cover. My boss didn't even mind paying for the damage out of park funds instead of making me fork over, which I thought was great.

Actually, the only time he got sore at me was when I ordered too much gas for the lawn mower, which was more his fault than mine. He figured I needed the responsibility of sending for my own supplies, and every Friday I had to fill out a requisition form for the gas I was going to be using the next week. But one time I got so distracted by a girl who was banking some significant assets inside a nickel's worth of fabric that I put the decimal for the number of gallons I wanted in the wrong spot, and I ended up sending off an order for ten thousand gallons.

When I got to work the next Monday, my boss was talking to the driver of a gasoline truck parked next to the lawn-mower shed. The truck was one of those jobs that blow you off the interstate, and I couldn't figure out what it was doing in the park until I saw that the requisition form the truck driver and my boss were handing back and forth was the one I'd filled out the week before. I would've explained about the sunbather if I'd gotten a chance, but my boss and the driver were taking turns yelling at me. When they quieted down, I mentioned how if everybody down at supply wasn't such a dope, they would've known a park could never use a truckload of gas. For a second the driver looked like he was going to take a poke at me. But my boss settled the guy down.

I wouldn't have minded all that hassle if I'd gotten anywhere with the sunbather that'd distracted me, but before I had a chance to go over and charm her to death, a guy showed up and from the way he started rubbing oil on her back, it was pretty clear they knew each other.

So math's not my favorite subject, and the class I got put in was for juniors who were pretty average and for some advanced sophomores. Allie Boggs was in that sophomore bunch, but she transferred out within a week, which I can't blame her for because a guy named Devaney teaches the class, and he's so in love with writing on the blackboard that even on the first day of school, he started right in doing problems. While he had his back to the class, a lot of us made paper airplanes out of Fielding's rules and flew them back and forth across the room. When Devaney turned around and saw all that air traffic, he got worked up and said a bunch of stuff about how he wasn't going to allow anybody to waste his time, which didn't seem fair considering how much of ours he was going to be wasting.

After math I went to Mr. Borkinson's room for history. You don't have to worry about his turning his back on you, because he sits on the front of his desk and gives ten million pages of notes, and if anyone stops paying attention, Borkinson lets them have it with a chalkboard eraser. I know he shouldn't do that but he does, and nobody's ever turned him in, because he never knocks you unconscious or anything. Actually, he's a pretty interesting talker who's been around to most of the places he's covering.

After history the day went by pretty fast, except for last-period PE, which is a stupid class. I mean, they send buses all over the place so we don't kill ourselves walking, and then at school there's a class to get us exercised. The only way out of PE is to be on a team, which is what I did my freshman and sophomore years, but I got sick of that. When you go out for a sport it doesn't matter to anybody whether or not you have a good time. It's like you're supposed to kill yourself if you lose, and I don't get worked up enough for that sort of thing. I just went out for stuff because it kept me in shape and impressed the hell out of girls. That's the sort of thing I'd never tell anybody in my family, because Dad'd give me a major speech about winning being a lifelong habit; Liz'd chew me out for trying to manipulate women; and Hank and Mom would go into mourning because I wasn't trying to find the true essence of sport.

I'm not saying I'm antiathletics. A lot of my friends are on teams and that's great, especially if they're girls, because it keeps them in shape and I really appreciate that. In fact, I can usually tell just by looking at a girl whether or not she's into sports, and I was surprised to see Allie Boggs in my PE class. So I walked over to her and introduced myself by saying how I only lived five blocks up the street from her.

"We're neighbors, almost," I said.

"Almost."

"And here we are in the same class."

"I guess so," Boggs said.

"I'm surprised you're here."

"Why?"

"I figured you'd be out for basketball."

"I have to take care of my sister after school."

"Emily?"

"That's right. Do you know her?"

"I think you yelled her name this morning when she attacked that kid on the bus."

I guess I shouldn't have brought that up, because Boggs looked uncomfortable, and to change the subject I asked her how she liked the neighborhood.

"It's fine. I went to the pool a couple times this summer, and I think I saw you there."

"I don't remember seeing you," I said. I don't know why I bothered lying, except maybe I wanted it to look like I went around being noticed by people that I didn't notice back.

After Boggs'd left I looked for someone I knew. Instead I saw Stratton and his bimbo girlfriend, which I couldn't believe because if the instructor started us off playing something like field hockey, Stratton'd cripple me. It turned out, though, that the class was going to play tennis for a month.

On the bus ride home I asked a girl who knew him if Stratton played tennis. She told me that he played all the time, which depressed the hell out of me. I pictured him hammering a shot into my face and my brain getting knocked out the back of my head.

If Hank'd been on the bus, I would've told him

how worried I was, but he'd been sent home early from school, which is pretty unusual on the first day unless you ralph up your lunch. Normally Hank has to be near death before he'll tell anybody he's sick, so I didn't count on him wanting to listen to me. That meant I'd have to talk to Mom. She's pretty good about not avalanching you with advice, but it turned out neither of them had time for me. They were in the living room talking when I got home, and you could tell Hank wasn't sick. So after saying hello, I stepped around the corner and listened.

"Mrs. Pauley was very upset," Mom said.

"I bet."

"She said the incident disrupted the class for the whole day."

"It happened after lunch, so it was more like half the day."

"She said it was your fault."

"Some of it was."

"Not all of it?"

"I don't think so."

"Who else's fault was it?"

"Do I have to say?"

"Was Emily Boggs involved?"

"A little."

"Mrs. Pauley said you and Emily and Seth Thompson were painting at a table."

"Emily and I were painting. Seth was showing off."

"How?"

"He was writing words on his paper and showing them to Emily."

"What kind of words?"

"The ones you've told me never to say."

"Did you tell Mrs. Pauley?"

"She was busy with Tommy Johnson."

"What was wrong with him?"

"Somebody'd bet him a dollar he couldn't drink his paint."

"Did he do it?"

"Mrs. Pauley thought so. The kid who bet the dollar said Tommy just poured the paint out somewhere when nobody was looking and smeared some on his lips."

"Couldn't you have waited to tell Mrs. Pauley about Seth?"

"He was really bothering Emily."

"How did you know?"

"I could see her paper, and she was drawing a pig that had Seth's face, and the pig was getting hit over the head with a chair just like the one Emily was sitting in."

"Did you warn Seth?"

"He laughed at me."

"Is that when—"

"No. I told him again to stop."

"And?"

"He called me one of the words he'd been putting on paper."

"So you dumped your paint onto his head?"

"Yes."

"What color was it?"

"I'd mixed a blue and yellow together and it turned out kind of green."

I was still hanging around the doorway to the living room, and it was a good thing Dad wasn't next to me to hear Mom talking about colors right after Hank'd been kicked out of school.

"I'm sorry if I got you in trouble with Mrs. Pauley," Hank said.

"Do you feel bad about what you did?"

"I feel bad I was taken out of school."

"Could you have done something else about Seth?"

"He won't stop unless you make him."

"Was he mad?"

"He didn't like Mrs. Pauley scrubbing him."

"She said he turned pink." Mom sounded like she thought Seth going from green to pink was funny, and she must've figured Hank shouldn't see her being amused, because she sent him out to the porch to wait.

When Dad got home and had been given an explanation from Hank about what'd happened, he let loose with a sermon about how it never paid to lose your temper, which is funny because Dad's the worst temper-loser I know. Hank didn't mention that, though, because it would've meant a lecture about interrupting would've been tacked onto the one he was already getting about temper control.

I didn't bother eavesdropping on their conversation, because I'd heard all of Dad's sermons before and the only interesting thing he could've talked about was Hank's punishment, but nobody'd find out about that until after dinner. Even if Dad figured it out before then, he'd keep it to himself until we'd eaten, which Mom hates because Dad comes up with some pretty weird punishment ideas.

By dinner that night Mom was worried enough about what Hank was going to get stuck with that she wasn't very friendly while she served up food.

"Peas or carrots, Elizabeth?" Mom asked my sister.

"Neither, Mom, I'm dieting."

"I'm sure you are, and I won't offer you dessert, but please take some vegetables."

"Carrots," Liz said, and her not arguing should've been a clue to me not to mess around with Mom, but I never catch stuff like that.

"Richard, peas or carrots?"

I'm Richard. I didn't mention my name before

because I don't like it. I mean, it's probably a great name for some guys, but not for me. I don't feel like a Richard. I don't know exactly what I do feel like, but definitely not Richard, because that's a guy in a suit who doesn't let himself get carried around on the bus the way I do. I could shorten my name, but I don't feel any more like a Richie or Rick than I do a Richard, so I'm stuck. Sometimes I come up with a name that I try to get everyone to call me, and while Mom was looking to unload some vegetables, I said, "Do you ever think of me as Clint, Mom?"

"I think of you as an eater of peas and carrots."

"Just try it once. Say, 'Peas or carrots, Clint?' "

Even though nobody'd asked him to, Dad got into the conversation right then and said how I'd been named after my grandfather.

"I know, Dad, and it's a great name for grandfathers, but it's not working out for me."

"Richard, will you please tell me if you want—"

"Peas, Mom."

"Thank you. William?"

William is my father's name and, boy, is he ever a William. I read a book last year for history about a French king named William the Conqueror who was so overmotivated, he ended up running England. Dad's like that, and I've got this theory that he named us kids for whatever English royalty we were supposed to model ourselves after, though if my name came from Richard the Lion-Hearted, things haven't worked out.

In a hundred years nobody's going to know if I ran around caring about everything or if I just had a good time. As far as I'm concerned, you might as well name kids after the Marx Brothers, because in the movies I've seen, those guys are smart enough not to take anything seriously. And using Groucho or Zeppo would make more sense than naming Hank after some English king who couldn't stay married.

I was thinking about that while Mom was dishing out dinner, and I would've asked Dad if he was going to be disappointed when Hank didn't get divorced six or seven times like Henry the Eighth, but before I could, Dad answered Mom's vegetable question: "I'll have carrots, Kate," he said like it mattered.

"Have you figured out Hank's punishment yet?" I asked, when the carrots were taken care of.

"We'll discuss that later," he said.

"Why not now?"

"Because we're having dinner now."

"Hank's so worried, he isn't going to be able to eat."

"He's already eating."

"That's so you don't feel guilty for punishing him."

"Why should I feel guilty?"

"Because Seth Thompson's a little monster who got what he had coming."

"Is that so?" Dad said, and I could tell he was getting sore, so to keep from saying anything else right then, I stuck some peas in my mouth.

When Dad saw he wasn't going to get interrupted, he said, "I'm glad you're concerned about your brother, because an hour ago I called Seth Thompson's father to arrange for Hank to paint something on the Thompson property as a way of Hank making up for what happened at school. Unfortunately, Thompson thought that would just give Hank another chance to dye his son, and while I was explaining that Hank wouldn't do something like that again, Thompson hung up on me. So I called the father of the little girl who'd been involved in the incident at school."

"You called Emily's dad?" Hank asked.

"I did, and at first he was just as reluctant as Thompson had been to put you to work. But I insisted that his daughter needed to see you weren't going unpunished."

"What did he say?" Hank asked.

"The only argument he made was that you were too young to work alone. That's when I offered to send Richard along to supervise."

"What?" I said, and a pea shot out of my mouth and just missed hitting Dad.

"Don't talk with your mouth full," Dad said while he was looking around to see where the pea'd gone.

"What's this supervision crap?" I asked him.

Dad turned back to me slowly, and in this cold voice he has he asked me what I'd said.

"Why do I have to watch Hank?"

"You're his brother."

"Isn't that punishment enough?"

"You're not being punished . . . yet."

I guess I lost my temper for a second, because I banged my spoon down on the table. That turned out to be a mistake because it startled Mom into flipping the chunk of meat loaf she was serving me into my glass of water. At first I thought the meat loaf would float because it's so oily, but it didn't. It sank to the bottom of the glass like a fish that'd gotten its head cut off, and just when I was going to mention that I'd lost my meat-loaf appetite forever, Dad told me to eat every bit I could scoop out.

It didn't help my mood any when Liz said she'd supervise Hank instead of me. I liked the idea, but it made me look like a jerk who didn't want to help his brother—which was true, but I didn't want it to be so obvious.

Dad made a big deal of thanking Liz for her offer but said how I was going to be doing some stuff at the Boggses—to keep from getting bored—that'd be too heavy for Liz to handle, which was a joke because my sister's thin and all, but she's got this sneaky strength you don't know about until you've insulted her and gotten smacked with a table.

CHAPTER 5

The next day in PE I asked Allie what I was going to get stuck doing while Hank painted. She said that if I wanted to get out of coming over to her house, she'd talk to her dad.

"Isn't there some heavy stuff I'm supposed to do?"

"You shouldn't have to do it just because your brother tried to help Emily."

"Did she tell you what happened?"

"My mom did. Emily doesn't like to talk about things like that."

"What's her problem?" I said, and I must've sounded sarcastic, because Allie clammed up, and she didn't have much to say to me until Friday of that first week of school.

On Friday Mr. Banks, the PE instructor, was done giving lessons and he was ready to set up the schedule for the tennis tournament he organizes every year. The tournament's supposed to fire everybody up to learn to play tennis, but it didn't me because most of the kids in class mainly tried to keep from knocking themselves out with their follow-through.

There were a few guys who knew what they were doing, and Stratton was one of them. In fact, that first week he did a lot of talking about how he wished there was somebody who'd give him some competition. Everybody thought he was a pain, but nobody got around to telling him to shut up. Actually, he was right about being unbeatable in singles, but doubles was harder to predict, because a bad partner can screw up anybody. I don't think he figured it that way, though, because he wanted his girlfriend for a partner and she was lousy—I mean as a tennis player; she was lousy as a human being, too, but Stratton didn't mind that.

Partners were arranged by a drawing, and on Friday I got paired up with Stratton's girlfriend. After they announced the names, Stratton headed for me, and I got my racket up in front of my throat, but when he got to me, he just said, "Let's switch."

"What?"

"You take my partner, and give me my girl-friend."

"Do I get any draft choices?"

"What?"

"It's a joke. Like we're trading minor league ball-players or something."

"Are you going to make the swap or not?"

"Sure, if Banks will let us."

"Arrange it."

"Who should I say my new partner is?"

"I already told you—you get who I have."

"Banks will want a name."

"Who's the girl on the bus with the sister as crazy as yours?"

"Allie Boggs."

"She's your new partner."

"I don't think she likes me."

"Neither do I, so what?"

"What if she won't be my partner?"

"Didn't I tell you to arrange the switch?"

"Yes."

"Did I say anything about wanting to help with the details?"

"Not that I remember."

"Then just do it."

"Right," I said, and while Stratton was walking away, I stood there hoping a car would smash through the fence that surrounds the school and run him over. I actually stood around for a couple minutes waiting for that to happen, but it didn't, and I finally went looking for Boggs.

I found her sitting on a bench, straightening her racket strings, which is usually something you don't see players doing unless they're halfway decent. But I didn't know for sure if she was any good, because during that first week I'd never watched her play.

"I'm really impressed with your playing," I said after I'd sat down on the bench.

"Thank you," Allie said, and even though she was looking at her racket instead of me, she didn't seem sore anymore over that crack I'd made about her sister.

"I think we'd do well if we were partnered up."

Boggs kept on arranging the strings, and for something to look at I watched while she did her repairs. At first I didn't pay a lot of attention, but then I started noticing that she held on to the strings longer than she needed to. And when she was done straightening, she'd run her hands over the racket, like she was wiping away some imaginary dust. In a weird way it was relaxing to watch somebody who didn't just touch stuff without paying attention to how things felt, and I sat there for a minute without saying anything. Boggs must've been wondering why

I'd come around, because she finally stopped fooling with her racket and said, "I've already got a partner."

"What?"

"Didn't you say you were looking for a doubles partner?"

"Not exactly, but you and I would make a pretty good team."

"I'm paired with Ted Stratton."

"Stratton?" I said, like I had no idea who he was.

"He's the one who punched you in the throat on Monday."

"Oh, Ted. That thing on the bus wasn't a punch. It was more like a chop. We're always kidding around. Yesterday I almost broke his leg while we were wrestling."

"What will he think of your taking his partner?"

"I'll square it with him."

"What about your partner?"

"What about her?"

"Won't she be disappointed?"

"I doubt it."

"You mean because she's Stratton's girlfriend?"

"You're kidding," I said, like I was shocked. "My partner is Ted Stratton's girlfriend?"

"That's right."

"Is that a coincidence or what?" I said, and I was going to lay it on thick about what a small PE class it was, but Boggs started staring at me like she knew I wasn't being straight with her. I might've been wrong about that, though, because she didn't say anything, and after a couple of moments she looked back down at her strings. It was getting late if Boggs and I were going to get a couple of practice games in, especially if she went back into the racket-repair business, so I asked her if she wanted to be my partner or not.

"I take this tournament seriously," she told me without raising her head.

"So do I," I said, and I wasn't kidding. I mean, just because a guy like Stratton destroys your Adam's apple and you don't have the guts to take a poke at him, doesn't mean you don't want to beat the guy some other way.

"Okay," Allie said, and she looked up at me and smiled. I would've apologized right then for having been sarcastic about her sister, except I figured it'd be better if I just didn't bring up what I'd said. Instead, I mentioned while we walked out onto a court that the next day was the first Saturday Hank and I'd be coming over. Allie told me again that she could get me out of that if I wanted, but I said I didn't mind doing it, which was a lie because on Saturdays I usually went down to the lake with some buddies. What we'd do is climb up onto the roof of a bathhouse and yell crazy stuff at girls who walked by—which sounds stupid and lifeguards were always chasing us off, but we never yelled anything that'd get us arrested. Mostly we tried to guess the names of the girls we liked the looks of and ask them if they'd go out with us.

But I didn't mention any of that to Allie; it wasn't her fault I had to watch my brother paint, and besides, once we decided to be partners, she was pretty anxious to practice. Not that she needed it. Everything she did on the court was so smooth that half the time I was embarrassed being out there with her; especially since a guy who'd transferred over from the same school as Allie told me later that tennis wasn't even her best sport—swimming was, which was hard to believe because when I'd seen her at the pool during the summer, Allie hadn't shown off the way I would've if I'd been any good in the water.

After we were done practicing, she said she thought we were well matched, which was just her being nice, and I didn't mind that the way some guys would've, because with Allie as a partner I had a chance at beating Stratton and his bimbo.

While Boggs and I were putting our rackets into their covers, Banks started blowing his whistle like he thought some kids had snuck off to India. Everybody headed for the shower, where so much towel snapping goes on, you're lucky to get dressed without having a leg amputated. Usually I hate that, but for some reason I was feeling pretty good that day, and I let some guys have it who I owed. You must've been able to hear their screams in the gym, because a coach showed up and gave everybody a lecture about how we might put somebody's eye out—which was dumb, because if you've ever been in a towel fight, you know that you're not aiming for anybody's eye.

CHAPTER 6

The next morning when Hank and I showed up at the Boggses' house, Mr. Boggs met us at the door and introduced himself. He seemed like a normal guy, so I figured Emily must've taken after her mom. But when we met her, she seemed okay. Actually, I was impressed by both parents, because adults usually think you're subhuman until you graduate from high school, and if they talk to you at all, you can tell it's real painful for them. But even though Mrs. Boggs looked like she had to get going to work, she asked if Hank and I wanted something to eat. Hank had some orange juice while I went outside with Mr. Boggs so he could show me what had to be done.

Allie was already in the backyard, and she looked embarrassed about having to use slave labor—which I think her dad realized, because he told me that if I'd changed my mind, Hank and I could go home.

"Thanks, but Dad would send us right back."

"I tried to talk your father out of this, but he was very insistent."

Mr. Boggs was looking at me while we talked, and to be polite I should've been looking at him. But instead I kept glancing at Allie, because she wasn't wearing any makeup and her hair was pulled into a ponytail so you could really see her face. Actually, I ended up checking her out a lot more than I should've, because she could've gotten the idea I was interested, and just because I noticed for the first time that her eyes were blue enough to go for a swim in didn't mean I wanted to ask her out—Dad says that eyes are windows to the soul, which I always thought was just another of his queer ideas that'd only make sense if you were falling in love, which I wasn't.

I'd been told the day before that if I asked Susan Cabot out she'd go, and Susan is one of the best-looking seniors in school. One time at the beach when she walked by the bathhouse my buddies and I were on, a guy named Joey got so impressed, he fell off the roof and landed right in front of Susan. You would've thought she'd get upset about Joey maybe breaking his neck, but she just stepped over him. Nobody really blamed her for that, because if you look as good as she does in a swimsuit, you can't stop to give first aid every time somebody crashes down in front of you.

Actually, I wasn't surprised she wanted to go out with me. She and Liz'd been friends once, and whenever Susan'd come over to see Liz, she'd seem amused by me. I even thought the two of them might've stopped being friends because of that. But when I asked Liz, she said it'd had nothing to do with me.

After Mr. Boggs had shown me what he wanted done, he and his wife left for work. She has a job in a museum, and Mr. Boggs runs a painting company, where I guess he's more or less the only employee. According to Allie, her dad does house repairs, too, though mostly he fixes stuff he's broken himself while getting ladders set up. I laughed about that and Allie did, too, but Emily didn't. She was hanging around like a pallbearer, and just to see if she was capable of smiling, I took the towels Mrs. Boggs had given us to use as painting rags and stuffed them under my shirt to get the muscular look Ted Stratton has. Then I strutted around and acted like I was chopping people in the throat. It wasn't a great impression, but Hank'd come out, and he laughed and so did Allie. Emily, though, just stared at me like I was an idiot.

"Do you know who I'm acting like?" I asked her.

"The one who bullied you on the bus."

"At least nobody got stabbed at," I said, because I didn't appreciate Emily's tone.

I figured she'd say something about how it was better to attack than be attacked, but she just got up from the back steps and went inside.

"What'd I say?" I asked Hank, but instead of answering, he went over and started to paint the garage.

"It wasn't your fault," Allie told me.

"Should I go apologize anyway?"

"I don't think she'd listen," Allie said.

"I'll give it a try."

Emily was in the living room sitting on the couch, and when I came up behind her and asked what she was doing, she spun around like I'd kicked her. That gave me another thing to apologize for, but before I could get going, she stuffed a bunch of photographs she'd been looking at into a box and took off.

One of the pictures fell on the floor, and I picked it up and was looking at how old it was when Emily showed up and snatched it out of my hand. She took off again and I didn't go after her.

"How'd it go?" Allie asked when I got back outside.

"It went all right."

Hank stopped painting and wanted to know what I'd said. He looked like he figured it'd been a mistake to send me to talk to Emily, so I didn't tell him anything.

"What was she doing?" Allie asked.

"Looking at old photographs."

"She collects them," Allie said.

"Why?"

"Why not?" Hank asked. You could tell he was wishing I'd quit wondering about everything Emily did. "Dad collects stamps, doesn't he?"

"But these are pictures nobody'd pay anything for. At least Dad could sell his stamps if he wanted."

"My sister wouldn't sell her pictures. She just keeps them in a box and looks at them when she wants."

"We have a book at home," Hank said, "with old pictures in it."

"Emily'd like to see it." I'm sure Allie'd meant in the future sometime, but Hank ditched his paintbrush and ran off toward home. That left Allie and me alone, and for something to say I told her that I hoped I hadn't made Emily cry.

"You didn't."

"How do you know?"

"She doesn't cry anymore."

Before I could ask what'd make a kid stop crying, Emily showed up, and she must've been eavesdropping because she said, "Allie cries at night in her room when she thinks no one can hear her."

"What would your sister have to cry about?" I asked.

I wasn't trying to pry or anything, even if it did sound that way. I was just putting Emily on the spot so she'd shut up. I figured Allie didn't want to listen to her sister tell a bunch of private stuff, and I was right, because Allie excused herself and went into the house.

The Boggs girls were starting to remind me of partners on a tag team, and when Emily was sure Allie was gone, she said, "Allie might cry about a lot of things that you're too stupid to understand."

"Like what?"

"Like teachers who make fun of her and girls who won't talk to her and boys who pick on her at recess."

I was going to ask when all this had happened, but before I could, Emily went into the house and left me sitting by myself. Without anybody to talk to, I started remembering how when my sister'd been fifteen, she'd cried a lot, too, except with Liz it hadn't been a private thing. She'd camped out on the living room couch and sobbed and choked and made gasping sounds that drowned out the TV no matter how loud I turned it.

"Are you worried about her?" Dad'd ask when I complained to him about Liz's crying.

"I'm worried about missing my favorite shows."

"I think you're more concerned about your sister than you're letting on."

"I'm worried about the TV, Dad."

"I think you need to help Liz."

"Don't make me do something weird."

"Why don't we make you responsible for checking to see if your sister's dehydrating?"

"What?"

"Do you know how to check for dehydration?"

"Why would I know that?"

"So you can make sure your sister isn't losing too much fluid."

"That's crazy. Liz isn't dehydrating."

"Have you checked her?"

"I don't know how."

"All you do is pull skin up from her arm. Then watch how quickly it falls back down when you release."

"Liz'd kill me if I fooled with her skin."

"Do you want to practice on me?"

"No," I said, because I thought that dehydration idea was just as dumb as Hank going home to get a book Emily wouldn't be interested in.

I turned out to be wrong, though, about what interested Emily. She came out of the house when Hank showed up, and the two of them looked through the book Hank'd brought. That meant there wasn't anybody out there besides me to go to work. I always feel like a jerk if I'm the only one working, so I went inside to get some water. While I was in the kitchen, Allie showed up and I felt uncomfortable because now that I knew she liked to cry, I was worried she'd start up around me, and I never know what I'm supposed to do. I mean, if it's your sister, you can ignore her, but if you do that with a regular girl, she'll think you're missing a heart; and if you try to pat her on the back, you're liable to get flattened—at my school just about every girl has a black belt, which is another reason I only go out with the older ones, because they're not as likely to go crazy and break your arm.

"I'm getting a drink of water," I said so Allie'd know I wasn't stealing a toaster or something.

"I'm sorry I ran off like that."

"Don't worry about it. Emily kept me company."

"What did she tell you?"

"How you hated it when teachers made fun of you."

"Teachers didn't make fun of me."

"According to Emily they did, and boys picked on you at recess."

"That's stuff that happened to her, not me."

I should've figured that out myself, but I never catch on when people are talking about one thing and meaning another—which makes me mad, and when Allie and I went back outside, I glared at Emily. She didn't seem to care, so I gave Hank the eye instead. He must've figured I wanted him to get working, because he grabbed his paintbrush and started slapping paint onto the garage.

He turned out to be the only one who went to work, because Emily kept looking through the book, and for over an hour Allie and I sat on the back steps talking about people at school. Finally she noticed the butterflies that were all over the yard, and because she's got a teacher who spends the first week of school talking about bugs, she was able to tell me what kinds were flying around.

For something to do I cupped my hands over my mouth so my voice'd sound like it was coming through a microphone and acted like I was in a control tower. I've seen a lot of airplane movies, and with Allie giving me the right names for what I was talking to, I did pretty well as an air traffic controller even if nothing did land where I told it to. I know that sounds stupid, but Allie and I got a kick out of it, and I think even Emily thought it was funny, though she was careful not to ruin her image by smiling.

Actually, I wasn't even sure she was paying attention until a starling flew into the yard and headed for the butterflies. Emily jumped up and tried to scare the bird, but the starling didn't pay any more attention to her than the butterflies had to me. In fact, one got stabbed out of the air right in front of Emily's face, and she got so worked up, she threw the book Hank had given her into the air so that the starling had to do some fancy dodging to avoid getting clobbered.

I suppose, with Emily throwing the book and all, I should've noticed how upset she was, but I didn't; and when I mentioned that I thought the starling was a pretty sharp flyer, Emily came over and gave me a kick that would've hurt like mad if she hadn't been wearing sneakers. Before Emily could find something harder to hit me with, Allie hauled her into the house.

Hank went and got the book out of the bushes it'd landed in, and after he'd wiped the cover clean, he came over and asked me what I'd been thinking.

"What do you mean?"

"Didn't you know how upset she was?"

"How did I know she hates birds?"

"She felt bad the butterfly was killed."

"Things die all the time."

"That doesn't make it right."

"Who says it has to be right?"

Hank gave me a look like he was wishing I'd been issued a brain, and I was going to say something sarcastic to him, but before I did, the Boggs girls showed up. Emily apologized, which you could tell was Allie's doing. I accepted the apology anyway, and right about then Mrs. Boggs got home. She didn't seem to mind that not much painting had been done on the garage or that the tree I was supposed to cut down was still standing. She even invited Hank and me to stay for lunch. I asked what she was going to fix, because a lot of mothers are weird cooks, and you wouldn't want to give their food to your dog unless you were punishing it.

Mrs. Boggs said she was going to make toasted cheese sandwiches, which was fine except a lot of families buy that processed stuff to save a little money—which I can understand, but I was hoping the Boggses weren't like that. Actually, I was pretty sure they wouldn't be, because while there weren't a million things around their house, what they did have was nice. So I wasn't surprised when Mrs. Boggs served us sandwiches made from Cheddar. After I was done with mine, I told her that the sandwich had tasted great.

"Thank you, Richard."

"You can call me Clint."

"Clint?"

"That's right."

"I thought your name was Richard."

"That's just the name I was born with. Most of the people who I know call me Clint."

"They do?" said Allie.

"Some do," I said.

"Mom doesn't," said Hank.

I started worrying that my brother was going to mention how I was just getting started with that Clint thing, so to change the subject I told Mrs. Boggs that I thought she had a nice kitchen. I could tell she appreciated that, and when Hank told her that the whole house looked nice, she said, "Thank you, Henry."

Hank hates it when anybody calls him Henry, but he didn't say anything because he probably figured Mrs. Boggs was confused enough by me being Clint instead of Richard. Instead of straightening her out about his name, he mentioned how he'd never seen a piano as big as the one the Boggses have in their living room.

"It's a baby grand my husband bought me when I started giving lessons," Mrs. Boggs said.

"Do you play?" Hank asked Emily, but instead of answering she buried her face in toasted cheese.

"She plays beautifully," Mrs. Boggs said, and you could tell she really meant it. In fact she sounded more impressed when she talked about Emily's playing than when she said how talented a pianist Allie was. That was surprising to me, because I figured Allie'd be the best at whatever she tried. And even though Mrs. Boggs hadn't meant to criticize, I went out of my way to say how Allie was a great tennis player.

"She's always been good at athletics, Clint," Mrs. Boggs said, and you could tell she was proud of Allie for other things besides piano playing. Allie didn't look any more comfortable being complimented than her sister did, so I changed the subject by bringing up the story of me and Liz popping mosquitoes, which I thought would be pretty interesting, but everybody stopped eating; and when Hank gave me a kick under the table, I went ahead and changed the subject again by saying how we hadn't gotten much done that morning.

"You can do better next Saturday," Mrs. Boggs said. I took that as a clue to split, so I got up and dragged Hank back home with me.

CHAPTER 7

By the second week of PE the instructor had finished his lessons and we
were getting ready for the tournament. The higher you finished, the
better your grade, though nobody exactly stayed
awake at night worrying about that, because you had
to be pretty desperate to care what you got in PE.

That didn't mean there weren't some kids pretty
hot to do well, because the whole school was invited
to the finals, and guys like Stratton were out to impress everybody with what great tennis players they
were.

You could tell, though, that Stratton was worried
about getting beaten in doubles, because he came
over to watch Allie and me a couple times. We actu-

ally played him and his girlfriend Dawn once in a practice match, and we thought it'd be close. But whenever Stratton came to the net, he'd look back to see what was happening on the baseline, which you're not supposed to do because it doesn't show much confidence in your partner. Plus if you're turned around at the wrong time, you might take a shot right in the face, which was what happened to Stratton. While the ball was bouncing off him and onto my side of the net, Stratton staggered around, and I would've called time out except I didn't know if his using his head was legal or not. So when the ball got to me, I played it, and Stratton got nailed in the head again.

Even though his pupils had rolled up out of sight, Stratton kept his balance and even managed to put his hands up in front of his face. To me it looked like he was getting ready to fight, but Allie said later that he'd been trying to protect his head. Either way Dawn should've had more sense than to come up and try to steady him, because he was so confused that when she grabbed onto him, he knocked her flat.

By the time Dawn got up, Stratton's mind had cleared, but instead of paying attention to the earful that she was giving him, he stared across the net at me. I thought about mentioning that only half the balls that'd clobbered him had been hit by me, but

Stratton didn't look interested in a recap of what'd happened.

When the match got going again, he chased down every ball I hit, and it didn't matter to him that he was stealing shots from his partner. You would've thought he'd have been more careful of her feelings after he'd decked her, but he wasn't; and when I hit a lob that should've been Dawn's shot, Stratton went back to the baseline and bumped her out of the way. I think she was fed up with that sort of thing, because while Stratton was stretching out to hit an overhead smash, she gave his stomach a serious poke with her racket.

He must've gotten the breath knocked out of him, because he sat down on the court and gulped for air the way a fish does in the bottom of a boat. Instead of hanging around to see if Stratton was all right, Dawn took off and she never came back. I guess she transferred to another PE class so she could avoid Stratton. She didn't even see him on the bus anymore because she started going out with a guy who delivered milk and he dropped her off every day at school in his delivery van.

Stratton being without a partner was no big deal, because the tournament was almost two weeks off and there were people transferring into class all the time who he could choose from; and the way it turned out, he didn't have to wait very long.

CHAPTER 8

The next day somebody told me Susan Cabot was going to transfer into PE so she could have a class with me, which I didn't believe for a second, because she's on the varsity swim team and could spend the whole year in study hall if she wanted. But she did show up seventh period, and after calisthenics she came over and said hello.

We had a pretty friendly conversation, and every time I told some stupid joke, Susan'd laugh like mad and touch my arm like she was having trouble keeping her balance—which she wasn't, and after a while she started to squeeze my arm more than touch it. I decided to go ahead and ask her out, but before I got around to it, she asked me who my doubles partner was. When I told her it was Allie Boggs, Susan said, "No, I mean, who are you going to play with in the tournament?"

"Allie and I do pretty well together, so I was thinking of staying with her."

"Even though I don't have a partner yet?"

"There's a lot of guys who aren't matched up yet."

"I'm not going to want someone just because they're available."

"No?"

"No."

"Who are you going to want?"

"Somebody who'll be willing to spend hours practicing with me." Susan gave my arm a pretty significant squeeze right then, and while I was thinking how she'd be a lot more likely to go out with me if we were tennis partners, Allie showed up. I introduced Susan, and I think Allie was going to say hello, but before she could, Susan said, "We've met."

"Where?" I asked, because Susan and Allie didn't exactly hang around with the same kids.

"Boggs finished second to me in the hundred meters at divisionals last year."

"I never congratulated you," Allie said, which I think Susan took as an apology, but it hadn't sounded that way to me. In fact, I was hoping

Susan'd be careful what she said to Allie. But she wasn't.

"Thanks for getting Richard ready for the tournament," she said.

"What do you mean?" Allie asked, and to change the subject, I mentioned how I thought I'd been poisoned by that day's school lunch, but nobody was listening to me.

"Richard told me you've been his doubles partner up till now," said Susan.

"Richard and I have been getting ready for the tournament," said Allie.

"I didn't think the teams were finalized yet."

"They're not, but most people know who they want to play with."

"Actually, so do I, don't I, Richard?" Susan looked at me and laughed like she was making a joke, but she wasn't, and what I should've done was just said straight out that I was sticking with Allie, but Susan was as great looking in a PE uniform as she was in everything else, so I laughed along with her.

"A lot of guys in this class don't care who they play with, so why don't you ask around?" Allie said.

Before Susan could say something back, Mr. Banks blew his whistle to get the practice matches started. Susan'd been assigned a court in the other direction from where Allie and I were headed, so she said good-bye to me and took off.

"Are we partners or not?" Allie asked while we were walking to our court.

"What are you talking about?"

"I'm talking about Susan Cabot."

"What about her?"

"Do you want to be her partner?"

"Why would I want that?"

"So you can get a date."

"Do you think I have to play tennis with Susan before she'll go out with me?"

"No, but you do."

"Is that right?"

"Yes."

"Maybe I've already asked her out and she's said yes."

"Have you?"

"Maybe."

"And maybe not," Allie said.

"Why don't we just get warmed up?" I said, but the team we were scheduled against never showed up, so we had to play a singles match against each other, and I got massacred. I mean, Allie didn't even let me win one game, and when the match was over, she split without saying a thing.

After I'd showered, I tracked Susan down and told her that I wanted to play doubles with her, but that I was afraid Allie'd commit suicide if I switched.

I could tell Susan didn't buy that for a second, but I asked anyway if she'd go to a movie with me the next night, and she said she would, which I couldn't believe.

CHAPTER 9

That was Thursday. Friday somebody phoned in a bomb threat just when the school's buses were arriving and we were taken to the football field, which has a fence around it, but not enough teachers came along to keep kids from wandering off, so school was finally canceled and whatever students they could find were taken home.

You'd think we'd have been happy about that, but nobody was who'd been at the school two years before, when the office's phones had been jammed every morning with kids making bomb threats. The administrators had always gotten everybody off the campus and tried to have things checked out fast enough to get classes going again, but all the public schools were having bomb threats, too, and there was such a waiting list for the bomb squad that it was usually noon before the buildings were declared safe. But by then most of the kids were off terrorizing the neighborhoods that surround our school.

The bomb squad searches never found anything, so the administrators finally decided to just check out things themselves without bothering to vacate the building. That plan worked until somebody claimed there was a bomb in the football equipment shed. That's such an isolated spot, nobody went to check out the call, and ten minutes later the shed blew up.

Instead of being grateful for all the free football equipment that'd landed in their yards, the neighbors complained so much that the administrators announced that from then on every day canceled would be made up during the summer.

That might not've been enough to stop the calls by itself, but the kids at school who were into drugs weren't interested in going back to having their lockers searched every day by the bomb squad, so word got around that the next kid to call in a bomb threat would answer to the dealers. That was a lot scarier than getting caught by the administration, because while the vice-principal could only think about throwing you out a window, the dealers would actually do it.

I don't mean to give you the idea there's a lot of drugs at our school, because there's not. We've got this policy where anyone caught possessing is permanently expelled, and normally that wouldn't bother most of the kids who do dope, but if you're expelled for possession, your parents don't get a tuition refund, and that's the sort of thing that really gets a lot of parents heated up. So there's probably less drug use around here than at most high schools. At least that's the impression the school tries to give, so it can attract kids who are into sports and academic stuff.

With school getting called off, Allie and I didn't get a chance to talk until Saturday morning. It was pretty clear when I saw her that she hadn't cooled off, and that worried me because we were going to need to communicate to win the tournament. Especially since Susan had told me Saturday night that she was going to be Stratton's partner. In fact, the whole date she kept telling me how interestingly primitive Stratton was and how he was unburdened by complexities, whatever that means. Mostly I tried to act like I wasn't bothered, but while she was giving me that complexity business, I mentioned that the only thing not burdening Stratton was a brain.

I'm sure Susan could tell I was upset. Susan's a good tennis player, and she would make Stratton pretty much impossible to beat.

Saturday morning when Allie finally did say

something, it was to ask me how my date had gone. You could tell she was hoping it'd been terrible, and actually it had been. But I didn't tell her that. I said I'd had a great time and didn't mention how upset Susan'd been when I'd showed up in my mom's Volkswagen instead of Dad's new Lincoln. I'd begged Dad to give me his car, but he was dressed up for a Shriners' meeting and said he couldn't go to something like that in a Volkswagen. I got sore and made a crack about Dad's outfit that I regretted right away, because I know the Shriners are okay guys who dress dumb on purpose.

Normally I would've gotten a sermon about how sarcastic I was getting, but Dad was late and he just told me we'd talk later, which gave me something to look forward to. I mean, I love hearing how I need to change my attitude in order to get ahead in a race I don't intend to enter.

When Dad's telling me that Junior Achievement stuff, I space out; in fact, I hardly ever pay attention to him, which backfires sometimes, and all the way over to Susan's I was wishing I'd put sheet metal over the hole in the floor on the passenger side of the Volkswagen the way Dad had been telling me to do for a month. It wasn't a huge hole you could fall through, but it was right where you'd normally put your feet, and if you didn't want them to dangle out of the car, you had to put your feet up on the dash. None of my buddies minded that, but Susan sure did.

She was wearing an outfit that had scarves and necklaces all over the place, and she made a big point of showing me how some of them were long enough to hang down through the hole in the car. I guess I didn't seem worried enough about that, because she told me about a dancer named Isadora who'd gotten her neck broken when a scarf she was wearing wrapped itself around the wheel of a convertible. I mentioned to Susan that the Volkswagen wasn't a convertible, but she said a hole in the floor was just as bad. And when I told her to put her feet up on the dash, she wouldn't take me seriously, so finally I just asked her to take her decorations off. She got so sore about me thinking her stuff had just been thrown on and could be taken off like a hat, that she ended up calling me a lout.

Susan never called you a dope or a jerk. It was always lout or boor or some other word you had to look up later—which I didn't mind, because I figured it'd improve my vocabulary. And I didn't mind her bawling me out, either, because I knew clothes were important to her, which was fine because she looked great Friday night. In fact, my temperature got raised about five degrees when I saw her, and it didn't go down at the R-rated movie we went to see.

Even though it was our first date, I started driving us out toward the Overlook when the movie let out, but Susan made me turn off into the mall and take her to an ice cream place all her friends hang out at. It took us forever to get out of there, and when I asked Susan if she was interested in going up to the Overlook, she said no.

"No?"

"Take me home."

"Already?"

"Yes."

"You don't want to go to the Overlook?"

"Maybe when you have your dad's car."

Usually cars aren't that important to girls, but I guess when they're all dressed up, they don't want to be hauled around in something they might fall through the floor of.

When I got Susan home, I walked her to the front door even though she said she could make it by herself. Actually, I had to chase her up the sidewalk, but when we reached the house, I got her turned around, and we were about to kiss when the door opened and Mr. Cabot stepped out. Instead of asking what an older guy like him was doing still awake, I straightened up like I was coming to attention. That's a queer way to greet anybody if you're not in the service, but Mr. Cabot kind of makes everybody feel like they've been drafted. Earlier that night, when I'd honked and was waiting for Susan, he'd shown up at my car window and told me to come into the house. Normally I don't do a thing just because someone wants me to, but Mr. Cabot's a big shot on the army base outside of town, and the way he gives orders you pretty much do what you're told.

When I got into the living room, I was introduced to Mrs. Cabot, and she gave me a smile and shook my hand but didn't say anything. While I was still shaking hands with his wife, Mr. Cabot said, "Susan tells me you're a junior."

"That's right, sir."

"Are you out for any sports?"

"This year, sir?"

"I'm not a student of history, young man. If I ask you a question, you can assume I'm referring to the present."

"I see, sir."

"So, are you?"

"Am I what, sir?"

"Out for any sports?"

"Not exactly."

"What does 'not exactly' mean?"

"It means no, sir."

While I was getting Mrs. Cabot to let go of my hand, Mr. Cabot asked me what college I was planning on attending and I said, "College, sir?"

"That's right, college."

"I'm still in the process of narrowing my choices."

"What've you eliminated so far?"

"Harvard."

"Harvard?"

"And Yale."

"What's wrong with them?"

"They won't want me," I said, and laughed, but Mr. Cabot just stared at me like he wasn't surprised.

Finally he said, "What are your plans for tonight?"

"With regard to college?"

"With regard to taking my daughter out."

"We're going to a movie."

"Which one?"

"I don't know yet. I thought we'd see what's playing and then go to the most military one."

Susan showed up right then, which was lucky because I was saying dumber stuff all the time, and in a minute Cabot would've canceled the date. Instead he escorted us to the door and told Susan to behave herself, which it turned out he didn't have to worry about.

So it wasn't the greatest date I'd ever had, and I would've been willing to complain to somebody about it Saturday morning, but Hank was painting the lower parts of the garage, Allie was working from a ladder, and Emily was sitting on the back porch waiting for someone to get thirsty enough for her to bring them water.

I could've sat around with Emily, but getting to work sounded better than that, so I grabbed the ax Mr. Boggs'd given me to cut down a dead tree on the alley side of the garage. Emily followed me over to the tree and I figured she wanted to help, so I told her that when trees fall, somebody's got to yell TIMBER. I said that I'd be busy checking wind direction and probably forget to yell, so it'd be a big help if she'd holler for me. I don't know if she believed that or not, but she kept out of my way, which was the main idea.

Mr. Boggs had asked me if I knew anything about cutting down trees, and I'd told him that I knew lots, which was a lie because all I knew was what I'd seen on late-night lumberjack movies where they show you a lot more about singing and kissing than they do about the lumber business. I did know that you're supposed to make a notch on the side opposite from where you were going to be cutting so your saw doesn't bind.

I probably should've realized, though, that things were different when you used an ax, but I didn't; and once I'd made the notch, I came around to the other side of the tree and started chopping. At first I figured a tree that'd been dead awhile would be pretty eager to fall over, but I was wrong, because it felt like I was chopping at the fender of a car. Whenever I took a break to give the ax a chance to stop vibrating, I noticed that Emily was frowning, but she always did that and I didn't think anything was wrong until Hank and Allie showed up.

They made me step back to look at how much the tree was leaning over the garage. And when Allie, Hank, and I tried to push it the other way, the tilt got worse. I figured maybe I had the whole notch thing backward and that what I needed to do was widen the notch on the garage side. I got Hank and Allie out of the way and let go with an opposite-side chop, which I knew right away was a mistake because the tree groaned and shook some of its limbs loose before collapsing onto the garage roof.

Nobody said anything for a minute, and then Hank mentioned that he thought Mr. Boggs'd had something else in mind.

"Is that a joke?" I asked.

"I guess," Hank said.

"You think it's funny that Mr. Boggs is going to kill me?"

"Dad won't get mad," Allie said. "He'll just let you know that you've let him down."

I would've said how that sounded worse, except Emily started clearing her throat. When she had everybody paying attention, she yelled, "Timber!" which was weird enough, but then when she was done doing that, she smiled. I'd figured her face wasn't set up for that but it was, and when Allie said, "Your timing's off," Emily and Hank started laughing. And even though nothing funny had actually happened, Allie and I cracked up too. The four of us had to sit on the ground, we got laughing so hard, and we kept that up until everybody was exhausted and lying back looking up at the clouds.

If you've never stared up at the sky, it's nicer than you'd think, especially if no one ruins it by talking, which no one did until Allie mentioned how her father was going to feel bad about the garage. That made me think of the time I'd helped Dad shingle our house, and when I mentioned how I might be able to fix the roof if there wasn't too much damage, Allie said we should try.

She got a couple of saws and climbed onto the roof with me, where we cut the tree into pieces that we tossed down to Emily and Hank. They hauled the tree parts out to the garage, and after an hour I could see there wasn't a lot of damage. While Allie and I sawed away the busted parts of the roof, Emily showed Hank were there was some plywood. When we had the roof ready, Hank cut the plywood into the sizes I told him, and Allie hauled the wood up to me so I could nail it into place.

There were some shingles inside the garage left over from the last roofing, and by the time Mrs. Boggs got home, we'd nailed them into place, put the tools away, and were sitting around looking beat.

I figured that if everyone kept their mouths shut, Mr. and Mrs. Boggs would never know about the tree, but in the middle of lunch Hank explained everything. When he was done, Mrs. Boggs laughed and said how she hadn't let her husband cut down the tree because she'd been afraid he'd drop it onto the garage.

After lunch we went to look at the shingling job, and even though there were a few rough spots, everybody said it looked good, except Hank, who said we'd done well considering we'd had to hurry.

"I don't think our having to hurry was that big of a problem," I said.

"Maybe not," Hank said.

"I think we would've done the same if we'd had a week."

"I guess."

"I don't see anything really wrong with the roof," I said.

"Maybe Mr. Boggs won't see how the shingles aren't totally straight," Hank said.

"I won't tell him what happened," said Mrs. Boggs, "and we'll see if he notices anything."

I appreciated her making it so I wouldn't get in trouble with her husband, but Hank said, "Can we stay until he gets home?"

"That won't be for hours yet, Henry."

"Is it okay if we wait?"

"No," I said.

"Emily could show us her photographs." Usually Hank's pretty good about not prying into people's private stuff, but he must've known what he was doing, because Emily said it was okay with her, and Mrs. Boggs and Allie looked as shocked as me but nobody said anything; instead we went into the house and sat down around the dining room table.

Emily came in with a box that she started taking photographs from, and while she spread her pictures out, she explained what they were of. That probably sounds like torture to have to sit through, but actually it wasn't, because the stuff she told us was interesting even though a lot of the photos weren't of the Boggs family, and Emily had to guess who the people had been from what was in the photo. For example, there was this picture of a family whose clothes were clean but worn out, and the father was bent over like he carried bricks for a living, but when I mentioned that brick-carrying thing to Emily, she said she'd always figured him for the owner of a cheese factory. According to Emily, it was only a small factory that the father worked by himself because he'd just come over from Switzerland and was having a hard time learning English. That was hurting the cheese business, so his kids were teaching him English at night as fast as they were learning it during the day at school.

That sounds stupid, but it seemed interesting at the time, and Emily probably would've gone on showing us her pictures all day if we hadn't heard something in the backyard, which turned out to be some neighborhood kids trying to steal tomatoes. The Boggs women were pretty surprised about that, but Hank and I weren't, because neighborhood kids are always stealing tomatoes to throw at each other. It's a dumb thing to do, but I'd done it when I was younger, so while I was chasing those guys off, I didn't exactly kill myself trying to catch them.

When I got back into the house, Hank was explaining about the tomato-stealing, except he was adding a bunch of stuff about how the kids never thought about the people who owned the gardens and how it must've felt to have your tomatoes stolen and your grapes eaten—everybody in our neighborhood has grapevines around their gardens, and the raiders don't carry off the grapes like they do the tomatoes, because you're not going to do much damage throwing a grape. What they do is eat as many grapes as they can while stocking up on tomatoes.

I was going to mention how the raiders never hurt anyone, but Emily said how there was an old lady down the street that'd gotten her fence destroyed the week before and that the tomatoes that hadn't been carried off had been smashed along with the old lady's grapevines.

There was a lot of headshaking in the Boggses' home over that, so I tried to lighten everybody up by mentioning that I'd run the guys off before they'd had a chance to do anything, but that didn't make any difference to Emily, because she packed up her photos and went upstairs.

Hank and I took off after that, and on the way home I asked him if Emily was in love with tomatoes.

"What?"

"What was she so upset about?"

"Those guys were going to steal stuff," Hank said.

"So?"

"So something happened once that made Emily afraid of people doing things like that."

"What was it?" I asked, and I figured it had to be something major to make Emily as weird as she was.

"She won't tell me anything except that someone died."

"Did someone dying give her a fear of modern clothes?"

"I think it's why she dresses like she does and collects old photos and can't stand to see someone be mean."

"If you're still talking about the tomato raiders, give it a rest. Those guys are just being kids."

8 1

"That doesn't make it right."

"Who says it has to be right?"

"Emily does."

"Then Emily's a dope."

Hank had been walking next to me, but when I said that thing about Emily, he stopped and asked in this shaky voice he has when he's mad, what I'd said.

"Forget it."

"Did you call Emily a dope?"

"I didn't mean it."

It was a waste of time apologizing to Hank, because he never wanted to hear it. Instead he jumped on me, and you'd think a nine-year-old wouldn't be much trouble in a fight, but Hank got holds on you that hurt like crazy. So while he was trying to get a grip on me, I gave him a shove that sent him into some bushes. After I'd checked to see that he was okay, I split, because he would've come right back at me if I'd waited around for him to get untangled.

CHAPTER 10

Monday in PE Mr. Banks explained a chart he'd made that showed you when you were going to be playing in the tournament and who against. The chart had all the possible matches, depending on who won and lost. When he'd put everybody to sleep with that, Banks explained that because he wasn't going to be able to referee every game, he was going to show us how to be line judges and referees. He even had another chart that showed which matches we'd be refereeing. After everybody'd given themselves a headache looking at that, we got marched over to a court where Banks went over a million things that might happen during a match and the calls we should make if they did.

When the guy was done, Stratton raised his hand, and I figured he was going to ask what the penalty was if one player accidentally killed another. But instead he wanted to know what happened if a judge made a bad call. Mr. Banks said that sort of thing was part of the game, but Stratton mentioned how there should be a way for a call to be overruled. You could tell Banks was wishing he had a chart that showed a schedule for getting things overruled, but he didn't, so he just told us that if anybody was really upset about a call, he'd talk to the referee involved and see if the guy wanted to change his call or remember the mistake the next time there was a close call to make. I could see that causing a lot of problems, but teachers never want to know what you think of their plans, so I kept my mouth shut.

It wasn't important anyway, because everybody could see that Stratton was just making it clear that anybody who made a call against him had better be ready to transfer to another school.

I don't want to bore you with the details of the tournament, but you should probably know that the doubles matches were going to be on Mondays, Wednesdays, and Fridays and that the singles were going to be on Tuesdays and Thursdays. The whole thing was going to take two weeks, with the singles championship on the last Thursday and the doubles the last Friday.

I wasn't worried whether or not I'd win the singles, because sooner or later I'd have to play Stratton, and I didn't have much chance of even living through that. I'd heard from a couple of people that he was still upset about losing the match to Allie and me, and I guess he was even more upset about me denting in his face.

I was glad when the bell finally rang, because with the charts and all, things were getting pretty complicated, and I resent it whenever I have to think in gym.

The singles matches got going the next day, and I played a guy named Lonnie, who'd been trying for two weeks to learn to hit a backhand. If you've ever played tennis, you know what a pain that shot can be, and you can't really avoid using it unless you stand in the corner and keep all balls to your forehand. But to do that you have to run like mad to cover the open court, which'll give you a heart attack if you try it for a whole match.

I'd played Lonnie once in a practice game, and even though he'd exhausted himself with that no-backhand business, I figured he'd try the same thing in the tournament. But he showed up carrying a racket in each hand, and when I asked him what he was up to, he said there wasn't any rule against using two rackets. I didn't believe him, so I yelled for the instructor, who came over without the rule book, which he wouldn't go back and get. Instead he told me to go ahead and play, which I was sore about until the match started, and I saw that using two rackets made Lonnie twice as bad as he usually was. He clubbed himself in the back of the head and smacked the rackets together, and halfway through the match he tossed one of the rackets over the fence and went back to his old, exhausting way of playing. When I'd beaten him, Lonnie couldn't even come up to the net to shake my hand, he was so tired, and I had to go over to his side of the court and pretty much carry him to the locker room.

CHAPTER 11

On Wednesday Allie and I had our first match. It was a real embarrassment, because we played a couple that ran around like they'd gotten themselves sewn together. Once when they were both up at the net, Allie hit a lob and instead of one of them breaking free and running back to take a whack at the ball, they just turned around so they could watch the ball come down. When it did, they laughed like the match was a joke.

We won 6–0, 6–0, which surprised me, because usually when the other team's helpless, Allie drops a couple shots outside a line to make the score respectable—she's better that way than I am, because I play the same no matter who I'm against, and I end up killing players like Lonnie and getting wiped out by guys like Stratton. But Allie keeps herself in low gear a lot, and I've actually only seen her fire up a couple times. It's interesting when that happens, because she gets an intense look and starts taking shots that should probably have been mine. After a point like that, Allie feels she has to apologize—which she doesn't, because I don't mind if it'll help us win.

And we were doing a lot of that. On Thursday I played somebody in singles who made two-racket Lonnie look good, and on Friday Allie and I won our doubles match, which meant that by the weekend I was still alive in two tournament categories.

Susan was in the same situation, and on our date Friday night all she could talk about was how Stratton was going to destroy me and how she was going to do the same to Allie. Susan was just as confident about winning in doubles, and at first I didn't mind her rattling on. But then I started getting depressed about how mad Stratton had looked after I'd hit him with the tennis ball.

Susan looked great again and we went to another R-rated movie, but instead of getting fired up, I kept picturing myself with tennis balls bouncing off my head, and I never got interested in the show. Especially since there were a couple of public make-out artists sitting right in front of us. They went at it through the whole movie, which was funny because they paid to see something they didn't watch except when they needed to come up for air. Even then all they saw up on the screen was what they were up to in the seats.

Susan decided to attach herself to my arm during the show, which normally I would've liked, but I wasn't in the mood that night.

After the movie I hauled her straight home, which you could tell she was surprised about. I mean, I'd brought the Lincoln and everything, but sometimes even if a girl looks great, you don't want her hanging all over you like you've grown another person. Not that I'm saying I'm this guy girls are attacking all the time, but I can still get bothered if Susan hangs all over me while she's explaining how Allie's going to get taught a lesson and that Stratton's going to kill me. So after the show I took her home, and you could tell she didn't appreciate that, but what did she expect?

Besides, I had to get some sleep Friday night because Mr. Boggs was getting a little concerned about the amount of work that was getting done Saturday mornings. He didn't say anything, but that Saturday he gave us a spray-painting machine that had so many gauges and valves, it looked like some kind of bomb.

Mr. Boggs went through detailed instructions I

only partly followed, but when he asked if I had any questions, I said I didn't.

After the Boggs parents had taken off for work, Allie and Hank and I took turns spraying the garage while Emily brought us water whenever we wanted it.

When the machine ran dry, I managed to get it taken apart, filled with paint and put back together without busting anything off. But when I went to start it up again, everybody looked worried, except the Boggses' basset hound, and it was asleep.

"Are you sure that's how the machine fits together?" Allie asked.

"It's exactly the same as it was before."

"Aren't those hoses hooked up to the wrong nozzles?" Hank asked.

"You're hooked up to the wrong nozzles," I said, because I resented being treated like an idiot. And when Hank started walking toward the paint sprayer to make some adjustments, I reached down and turned on the thing.

Right away I knew I'd made a mistake, because the pressure valve shot open, and the machine started hopping around the yard, dragging its hoses behind. I chased after it, trying to get my hand on the power switch, but just as I did, the top of the machine blew off, and everything in the yard got painted white, including the basset hound.

I get distracted by funny things sometimes, and even though I was pretty upset about having blown up Mr. Boggs's equipment, I started thinking that the Boggses' dog had probably died a long time ago, and the Boggses couldn't get themselves to tell Emily; instead, they'd had the animal stuffed and were moving it around to different spots. Just so I'd know for sure, I went over and shook the hound. That's the sort of thing some animals don't appreciate, but all the basset did was open its eyes, look at its fur, and then at me.

While everybody else hosed down the backyard, I cleaned the dog, which kept me from running around and stomping on whatever parts of the machine I could find. By the time I was done, the paint on me had crusted up, and I looked like one of those cookie men Mom bakes at Christmas. Frosted the way I was, I couldn't get away when Allie sprayed me with the hose, or when Hank and Emily scrubbed me with the brushes they'd been using to get the paint off the lawn furniture. It wasn't until I was pretty much out of skin that they figured I was clean enough to be laid out in the sun next to the basset to dry.

I actually fell asleep, which was surprising, because I hadn't been doing much of that since I'd realized Stratton and I were both heading for the singles championship. I didn't mind so much the idea of him humiliating me—I was used to that sort of thing—but I didn't like the way it was going to be in front of the whole school.

Stratton and I each needed one more win to reach the championship, and I was so worried, that whenever I did sleep during the night, I ended up dreaming that Stratton and I were Roman gladiators —in my dream we fought with tennis rackets and I was always at a disadvantage because the spectators kept pelting me with tennis balls.

But for a little while in the Boggses' backyard I was lying in the sun next to a dog, which was kind of a calming thing, and I slept until it was time for Hank and me to go home.

CHAPTER 12

On Monday Allie and I won again, and I should've been on top of my game for the singles match on Tuesday, but I wasn't. At least, not after I walked onto the court and saw that one of the line judges was Stratton. Having him on the court made me so nervous, I lost the first two games without scoring a point.

During the third game Stratton called some of my shots in that weren't, and I started figuring he didn't want me to lose before he had a chance to humiliate me. His being on my side was like a reverse challenge, and I started hitting shots that Stratton couldn't call in unless he wanted a referral to the school nurse for an eye exam.

When I lost the match, I wasn't broken up like you'd think a guy would be who was out of the singles competition. In fact, by getting myself eliminated, I could concentrate on doubles, where I'd at least have a chance.

The next morning while Hank and I were waiting for the bus, he asked if the other guy'd been better than me.

"What other guy?"

"The guy who beat you in tennis."

"I don't know if he was better or not. He just got more points."

"Had you played him before?"

"In a practice game."

"Did you win?"

"What's with all the questions?"

"Liz thinks you lost on purpose."

"Why would I do that?"

"So you wouldn't have to play in the championship."

"That's stupid."

"You played your best?"

"It's a school tournament that doesn't mean anything, so what difference does it make how I played?"

Hank looked off down the street like he was hoping the bus would hurry up and not make him stand around with someone as disappointing as me. That made me sore and I said, "I'm getting tired of you expecting me to do stuff perfect all the time."

"I don't expect you to be perfect."

"Yes, you do. And it's not fair, because you like a lot of things that are all screwed up."

"Like what?"

I would've mentioned Emily, except I didn't want to get attacked again, so I mentioned the Mustangs, who're a minor league ball club that plays in our town. They're only single-A, which is the lowest level, and they make a million mistakes, but that doesn't bother Hank.

"Do you know why I go see the Mustangs?" Hank asked.

"Do I care?"

"I go because they're never bad on purpose."

"So?"

"So they do the best they can every game."

I was praying the bus would come, because Liz was due to show up, and she would've gone ahead and said a lot of things Hank was just hinting at. The two of them have a lot of the same ideas; in fact, Liz is the one who takes Hank to the Mustang games even though she hates baseball. Actually, it bothers me a little that they're pals, because I'm Hank's older brother, not her.

Once last summer I asked him if he wanted to go to the beach and swim while my buddies and I tried to pick up girls. He thought I was kidding, and by the time he figured out I wasn't, I'd changed my mind. Even though he said he wanted to go after all, I told him to forget it. You could tell he felt bad about that, but a lot of times I ended up saying something to hurt him because it's the only way to get him to leave me alone—which is what I did at the bus stop: "Maybe I did lose on purpose, but if I did, it's none of your business. And if the same thing happens Friday, that won't be any of your business either."

Liz walked up to us right then, and I was set to ignore her, but the bus came. When I got on, I sat as far away from the two of them as I could, because I wasn't interested in their sports commentary. Especially since Liz's boyfriend is on the school's tennis team and she probably figured watching him practice made her an expert. Liz never actually talked about tennis, even though she was always getting her journalism teacher to let her go out last period to cover the athletic field beat. That's what she called it— "the athletic field beat." But instead of researching stories about the football team's practices, Liz'd watch her boyfriend do conditioning drills. And when Matt wasn't stretching his muscles out, he'd sit around in the stands with Liz and check out the PE tournament.

They were in the stands Wednesday when Allie and I were scheduled for our semifinal match. We were supposed to play a team that'd been going together since birth, but the pressure of the semifinal must've gotten to them because they started arguing during calisthenics, and while the instructor was trying to get them settled down, I mentioned to Allie that it was lucky we weren't interested in each other, because it might foul up our teamwork. Instead of answering me Allie walked off, and when our opponents went ahead and forfeited, I got stuck refereeing a consolation match.

It was the first match I'd had to referee, which meant that instead of being a line judge who just decided if a ball landed in play or not, I had to keep score and settle disputes and be generally in charge of things. That's not my strength.

Once during the match somebody got clobbered pretty bad up at the net, and their partner came running up to me and said, "Did you see that?"

"No, I'm blind," I said.

"What are you going to do about it?" the partner asked.

"I'm considering surgery," I said.

I was only trying to lighten the mood with a stupid joke, but the partner took a swipe at me, and it was a good thing I wasn't refereeing the championship match the next day between Susan and Allie.

Both of them had blown through the qualifying

matches without being challenged, though Allie's winning margins had always been lower than Susan's. That shouldn't have made Susan as confident as it did, because Allie just wasn't into running up the score on people, but I didn't try to tell Susan that. In fact, I was secretly hoping she'd lose. I know that's weird considering I was going out with her, but Susan'd already won so many trophies, her house looked like a high school hall of fame.

On Thursday I walked with Allie over to the court, and while I was telling her to follow through with her swing and a couple other things she already knew, Susan showed up and wanted to kiss me for good luck. I told her we'd get in trouble, but she said the PE instructor hadn't shown up yet. Before I could mention how the bleachers around the court were getting crowded, Susan gave me one of those long kisses that you'd suffocate during if a cold was plugging up your nose.

By the time we got separated, Allie'd walked off, and some of the girls in the bleachers were yelling at me to come and sit by them. There were even some guys who thought they were funny who hollered for a kiss. I got off the court quickly and was so anxious to find a seat that I took the first empty one I could find, which was right next to my sister and her boyfriend.

"Does Susan always loosen up her lips like that before a match?" my sister asked.

I just ignored her, so Matt said, "Is Boggs ready to play?"

"How should I know?" I said. "She never talks to me."

Matt and Liz must've figured out I wasn't interested in chatting, because they left me alone, and I was able to join most of the other guys in the stands who were watching Susan warm up in a tennis outfit that didn't have nearly the coverage of a PE uniform. I don't know if she'd lost her uniform or what, but none of the guys I was sitting near complained, because Susan was pretty exciting to watch even before the game got going. In fact, she was more fun to watch before the game than during—looking great didn't do her much good against Allie. I'd never seen my partner play as well as she did that day, and Susan spent most of the match chasing after balls beyond her reach. Even when she did manage to return a shot, Allie was at the net to hit a winner.

The match got so one sided, nobody bothered to clap even though Allie was playing great. I was pretty excited about the way things were going, and I should've cheered a little, but I figured if I did and Susan saw me, Dad would have to buy a Rolls-Royce before I'd get another date. So I sat through the whole match without saying a thing except when my sister asked me if I was surprised.

"About what?"

"I didn't know Allie was that good," Liz said.

"Neither did I."

"Susan hasn't got a chance."

"Hank would love to see this," I said.

"Why?" asked Liz.

"He's a nut about people getting it right."

"Do you think that's what Allie's doing?"

"Don't you?" I asked.

"I don't think she should be trying to embarrass Cabot."

"Maybe she's evening things up from when Susan beat her at a swim meet."

"Is that what you think?"

"Why else would she want to win this big?"

"Never mind," Liz said.

The match ended right then, and I went down to the court. As Susan came off, I told her I thought she'd played hard, which was about the only good thing to say. She stopped and stood there in her wilted outfit and said, "Your partner is going to regret that."

Before I could ask what she meant, Susan took off—which was fine, because I wanted to congratulate Allie. But when she came along, I had to more or less tackle her before she'd let me tell her what a great game she'd played. When I was done, Allie pushed by me without saying a thing, and maybe her acting more upset than Susan makes sense to you, but it didn't to me.

CHAPTER 13

After that I kept thinking how much trouble the tournament was turning into, and that it'd get worse if Allie and I won in doubles the next day. I even started figuring I'd be doing Allie a favor if I went ahead and made us lose. I mean, Cabot'd get over having lost today, but if she got beaten tomorrow, too, Allie wouldn't have a future at our school. I ended up being wrong, though, about how much losing Susan'd put up with—because the next morning in the halls everybody avoided Allie, and in homeroom somebody told me Susan'd been spreading it around that Allie'd said the sports program at our school sucked. According to Susan, she and Allie'd had this big argument in the locker room after the match and Allie'd cut down our school pretty bad. I didn't believe that and I don't think anyone else who knew Allie did either. But Susan's pretty popular, and everybody acted like she was telling the truth, which must've made Friday morning hard on Allie.

I know I should've helped out by walking Allie to class, but that sort of thing is murder on your reputation. So I stayed clear of her until noon, when I decided to see what she'd think of not killing herself to win the tournament that afternoon. I mean, according to Dad I should see problems as challenges, but my eyesight's better than that, and if there's a way to avoid a hassle, I take it.

I decided to talk to Allie in the cafeteria, because it's always crowded there and you don't stand out, but Allie was by herself at a table that looked like a lunchroom island, and when I saw how out in the open she was, I would've turned around, except she saw me. I figured it'd kill her if I'd ditched out right then, so I went over and sat down with my tray.

I said hello and she said hello, and I must've looked uncomfortable, because Allie asked if I was worried about being seen with her.

"Why would I be?" I asked.

"Your girlfriend's put me off limits."

"I don't care about that. And besides, I don't have a girlfriend."

Allie just looked down at the salad on her plate

and poked at a couple of croutons, so I asked her if she believed what I'd said.

"No."

"Why not?"

"Because it's not true."

"Is that right?"

Allie kept her eyes on the salad, but she did nod and I said, "Do you want to know what I think the truth is? The truth is that this tournament is screwing everything up, and I'm wondering if it's worth it."

Allie looked at me and, in a whisper almost, asked me what I meant. I told her I thought things would be a lot easier if we didn't win that afternoon, and for some screwball reason Allie stood up and she said, "My parents are coming to watch, and I'm not going to disappoint them so you can get a date."

I reached across the table to get Allie back into her chair, but she pulled away and started to cry. I was hoping no one but me would notice, but the cafeteria has these high-powered lights that make the place like the surface of the sun—which is fine if you're trying to tell creamed corn from macaroni and cheese, but the brightness made it impossible for Allie to cry without everybody in the room noticing.

I could understand her being high strung the day of the championship, and I felt like going over and wiping away her tears, but I knew I'd get socked for sure if I tried that, so I stayed were I was.

When Allie'd gotten her crying stopped and had sat back down, I said, "Just because we lose doesn't mean you won't have played well. Stratton could have a great game, or Susan even."

"I'm not worried about how anyone else plays."

"You can't ignore what other people do."

"I'll let you worry about other people."

"What does that mean?"

"It means I thought we were friends."

"We are, sort of."

"No, we're not. Not even sort of. A friend wouldn't have ignored me all morning just because somebody who thinks she should never be beaten got mad."

I started to tell her she was overreacting, but instead of listening she got up and walked over to the conveyor belt that carries dishes back to the kitchen. At first I thought Allie was going to climb onto the belt and let herself get dishwashered to death, but instead she scraped her plate and set her glass and silverware where they were supposed to go. Then she walked out of the cafeteria as calmly as you can with everybody staring at you.

After Allie was gone, I figured somebody'd come over to congratulate me, but no one did, which fine. I felt lousy about what'd happened, and I started wishing I'd taken meat instead of fries, because then I'd have had a knife to stab myself with. But forking myself to death sounded pretty unpleasant, so I sat there like an idiot until my sister showed up. She sat down and slid her chair next to mine like she was going to share my fries. But what she was really doing was getting close enough to explain privately what a jerk I was. I kept my mouth shut while she told me how I was going to go with her to find Allie and apologize for whatever it was I'd done.

When Liz took off, I dumped my tray and followed like I was on a leash; but Allie'd disappeared. When we couldn't find her anywhere in the school, we checked with the office, and they told us that she'd gotten permission to leave for a couple hours. You couldn't blame her for that, because there's nothing like a lunch-hour humiliation for distracting a player who should be getting psyched up for a championship match.

Seventh period, on my way to PE, I saw Susan in the hall, and she must've heard about what'd happened in the lunchroom, because instead of looking worried about what a tough team Allie and I were going to be to beat, Susan gave me a stupid little wave like everything was forgiven. I should've talked to her, but when I'm nervous I don't concentrate very well during conversations, so I just headed for the locker room. Stratton was there getting dressed, and he gave me a wink that made me want to throw up. Actually, I'd felt like throwing up all afternoon, and I was half hoping I would, because then I could've gone home, but I didn't. Throw up, I mean. You never do when you want to.

When I'd gotten changed and onto the court, I couldn't believe how there were twice as many kids in the bleachers as there had been the day before—I know there's a lot of athletes who get turned on by a crowd, but not me. I'd play at some secret location if I could, so the idea of having most of the school watching made me so dizzy that while Stratton and Susan did some screwball stretching exercises, I sat on the bench and waited for Allie to show up— which she didn't do until right before the match. I thought we might have a last-minute conference, but she walked right by me and onto the court. She was probably worried that I'd try to talk to her again about that stuff I'd brought up at lunch, but she shouldn't have been. I was so unnerved by having gotten myself into a spot where I was going to be playing an important part, that nothing Allie did would be enough to help us win. I mean, I see myself as an in-the-background kind of guy who stands around and says "This will never work" a lot, and it wasn't until I saw all the kids in the stands that I realized what I'd gotten involved in.

During the time they give you to warm up, I

couldn't get my hands to stop sweating and my racket continually slipped out of my grasp. It got so bad that a lot of the kids in the stands started laughing like I was some kind of comedian who'd greased his racket up and was going to be chasing it around all afternoon. Allie ignored me during the warm-ups and just tried to keep from getting hit by my racket, and she didn't say anything to me until the warm-ups were over and Mr. Banks called out for one member of each team to come up to the net for a coin toss. "You do it," Allie said.

"My hands are so slippery that if he wants me to catch the coin, we'll be here all day," I said as a joke, but Allie just turned and walked back to the baseline.

Stratton came up to the net and he held out his hand so we could shake, like he was this great sportsman, when what he really probably wanted to do was get his hand washed. After we'd shaken, Mr. Banks tossed the coin in the air and told me to call it, but I didn't, because while I was watching it flip around, the coin was silhouetted by all the kids in the stands at the far end of the court.

And my brother was in those stands. I saw him sitting there surrounded by high school kids who'd toss him out onto his head if they wanted his seat. But he had a big smile on his face like he wasn't worried a bit about that or about getting suspended for sneaking out of his school, which is what he must've done.

I know there's a lot of guys who would've gotten fired up about people from his family showing up, but it made me mad. I knew Hank was there because he thought I might hit a perfect stroke that'd win the match and put him into some crazy harmony with the universe. And even if he wasn't thinking about some goofball thing like that, I resented his showing up and making me feel that if things didn't go right I'd let him down. That's what I really hate about making the big-deal kind of effort that Dad's always talking about—if it doesn't work out everybody's real polite and says how you gave it your best, but what they're really doing is feeling sorry for you.

I was thinking all that stuff while the coin toss was going on and, when the thing landed I looked down at it and said, "Heads." Mr. Banks and Stratton looked at me like I was the dumbest cheater they'd ever seen.

"I just mean it landed heads," I said. "I didn't mean I was calling it heads."

"Then you wanted tails?" Stratton said.

"I don't know what I wanted," I said.

"Am I supposed to toss it higher to give you more time to decide?" Mr. Banks asked, because he's kind of a sarcastic guy.

"I just forgot to call it," I said. "Let's do it again."

"Why should you get two chances?" Stratton asked.

"Fine. You serve first. It doesn't matter to me." And it didn't. Who served first wasn't crucial and I was too mad about Hank showing up to worry about coin tosses. In fact, I was so sore at Hank that I stopped being nervous.

That wasn't any help, though, when Stratton started the match, because he's got a bullet serve that I was helpless with the first time we played him. Even Allie'd only hit a return half the time in the earlier match, and she didn't manage even that in the first set of the championship, which we lost six games to none.

I was actually playing okay and balancing out with Susan, but Allie was off her game. If you'd never seen her play before you wouldn't have thought she was bad or anything. In fact, against anyone else we would've been winning, but against Stratton and Cabot we were halfway to losing the championship.

During the break they give you before the second set, I asked Allie if she was okay. She said she was, but her voice sounded shaky, and when I asked her what was wrong, she walked back onto the court without answering me. I would've followed if my sister hadn't shown up behind the bench I was sitting on. When I told Liz that she'd picked a bad time for a school-paper interview, she said, "I just wondered if you knew why you were losing."

"It's not my fault, if that's what you mean."

"That's not what I mean."

Mr. Banks was waving his arms around to signal everyone that it was time to get the slaughter going again, so I said to Liz, "Do me a favor and get out of here."

"Somebody's already doing you a favor, Richard," she told me, and took off.

I don't know if you remember me saying how I hate it when people don't say exactly what they mean, but I do. And while I was walking back onto the court, I kept looking over my shoulder at Liz and wondering what she'd been talking about.

On a tennis court if you're not watching where you're going, you're liable to run into your partner, which is what I did. I excused myself, but Allie didn't say anything back, and when I looked at her, I could see she was crying in a low-level way you had to run into to see. It wasn't until then that I realized Allie was throwing the match.

I should've been happy about that, but I wasn't, because once Mr. Boggs'd told me that Allie wasn't out for any teams at school this year because whenever she lost at something, she'd walk around looking emptied out for a week. I guess he'd finally decided it'd be better if Allie stayed clear of competition until she matured a little more, and when I saw her crying during the tennis match, I figured the Boggses hadn't gone far enough and that they should've banned Allie from PE too. Or at least made sure she didn't end up with a jerk like me for a partner.

I was standing there feeling so lousy about what was happening that when Susan served to me, I smacked the ball back at her as hard as I could, and she had to make a goofy leap to get out of the way. I don't know if she felt worse about looking uncoordinated or about me scoring a point, but either way she was upset enough to double-fault her next serve, which means she missed on both attempts at getting her shot in and lost the point. That's unusual for her. Her serves aren't fast, but she gets all stretched out and reaches her racket way back the way you're supposed to so that she gets a lot of serves past guys who are busy watching her form.

But Susan's stroke had gotten messed up, and she double-faulted two more times, which gave Allie and me the game. You could tell Stratton was about to have a heart attack over that, but he was smart enough not to say anything to his partner.

I served next and I got into a groove where I didn't have to worry about my follow-through or what position my feet were in—sometimes things take care of themselves without having to be thought about, and I'm usually a lot better off when my mind doesn't get involved. That's what happened during the second game, because my serves were wicked things that were hardly ever returned, and when they were, I charged the net and hit a winner.

We won 45–0, and if you haven't played tennis you're going to think we played forty-five points when actually we'd only played four. In tennis you give yourself fifteen points the first two times you score; the third time's good for ten and the fourth for five. So the scoring goes 15 to 30 to 40 and then 45. I know that's crazy, and I think they just did it that way so it'd be impossible for little kids to figure out the game and start hogging the courts.

Stratton served the third game, and they beat us after a bunch of what're called deuce points, which just means the game was tied a lot.

During Allie's service game I was at the net most of the time. Usually that's something I want to avoid, because I end up getting hit with the ball a lot more than you're supposed to. But during that game I was standing in the right places and chopping back winning shots like mad. We won easily, even though Allie's serves weren't the best I'd ever seen her make.

Down three games to one, Susan had to serve again, and you could tell she was trying to work her serve back into shape, because she did everything in slow motion the way you do when you're first learning. Her first shot was long, but it looked like she was figuring things out, and her second shot barely missed. She probably would've gotten her next one in if Stratton hadn't gotten fed up and walked back to tell Susan to get her butt in gear. That's not the sort of thing she hears much of, and you could tell she didn't like it because she hit her next serve over the bleachers. When Stratton started back toward her again, Susan hit a rocket at him that he had to drop to the ground to get out of the way of, and he pretty much stayed there while Susan double-faulted the rest of the game away.

It was my turn to serve and we won, but it was close because I was losing that groove I'd been in. There was nothing I could do except hope I kept enough of the touch to win the set. But Stratton took care of that by getting as crazy as Susan and knocking his serves twice as far as she had, which tied up the match at one apiece.

During the break before the last set, Stratton and Cabot cooled down enough to talk to each other, which was depressing because I wanted to win, and it didn't have anything to do with showing Stratton up. I can't tell you exactly what it did have to do with except I wouldn't have minded showing Allie I wasn't as big a loser as she thought. But while Stratton and Cabot were taking blood oaths to lay off the home runs, Allie sat as far away from me on our bench as she could. And when I said how I thought we had a chance, she told me to save the act.

"What act?"

"That you want to win."

"I do want to win."

"You don't know how."

I know Allie was upset, but that don't-know-how business made me sore, and I said, "I'm not going to kill myself if we lose, the way you would, but that doesn't mean I'm not trying."

Instead of answering Allie got up and started back onto the court. But I blocked her way and said, "I'm sorry I ignored you this morning and was a jerk at noon, but I'm not kidding about wanting to win."

Allie stared at me and I probably should've been watching her racket to see if I was going to get smacked, but instead I looked at Allie's eyes and noticed again how blue they were.

Mr. Banks yelled at us to get going, and when the last set started, I could tell I'd lost my touch. But Allie started playing hard and the match stayed so close that Stratton got desperate and tried to get an edge by giving the guys who were refereeing a hard time. That made me sick, because why bother winning if you're going to do it that way, but I guess guys like Stratton—and even Allie, from what I'd heard— are out to win no matter what. Not that we were getting cheated out of any games, because there weren't any close calls during the set. It ended up tied at six games apiece, which meant that there had to be a tiebreaker to decide the championship.

Susan served first and when I messed up a shot, Stratton came to the net and congratulated me. He stayed up close while Allie prepared the serve, like he'd decided she couldn't get anything by him. But instead of her usual stroke, Allie used a shot I'd never seen before, and when the ball hit, it took a crazy bounce past Stratton.

Allie aced Susan the same way, but that lead only lasted until Stratton scored twice off his serves and I lost both mine. In tiebreakers the scoring isn't screwy, and we were behind two points to five. Seven points are needed to win as long as you're leading by two, which meant we couldn't lose another pair of serves, and we didn't because Allie went to the net twice to hit winners and then used her spin serve to put us ahead 6–5.

We were only one point from winning, but it was Stratton's turn to serve again, and he got off a great shot that had all sorts of topspin on it. The ball bounced high to Allie's backhand so that I thought she'd just chop a return over the net where Susan'd have an easy play. But instead Allie swung through the ball as hard as she could and drove a shot straight down the line that cleared the net and flew back to the corner. Stratton dove to try and make a play but he was too late, and when the ball bounced away without being touched, I tossed my racket into the air because we'd won.

The racket carried back toward Allie, and I thought she might catch it for me. But she was too busy watching a linesman and just as my racket landed a couple feet behind Allie, the linesman yelled, "Out!"

It had to be the latest call in history, and I couldn't believe the guy'd made it. Neither could anyone in the stands, and a lot of people started booing. The referee came out onto the court to talk to the linesman, but the kid refused to change his call. Finally Banks came over to Allie and me and said how he was trying to teach responsibility and wasn't going to overrule anybody. I guess that was supposed to make us feel better, but it didn't, and I said that at least he could have us play the point over.

When Stratton heard that, he came up to the net and warned me to pipe down, but I didn't and neither did the crowd.

In tennis you can refuse to play if there's too much noise, and that's what I did. Banks had to get out a megaphone and yell at everybody to settle down. That just made the crowd noisier, and when some kids started throwing things at the linesman, Allie told me to get back and receive the next serve. I tried to explain to her that if we refused to play, we'd get another chance at winning off her return, but she didn't want to hear it. So with the score tied I went back and got served a bullet by Stratton that I barely managed to return over the net. Susan put the ball away with a pretty good shot, and she probably expected the crowd to applaud like mad, but all they did was stop booing.

With us one point from losing the match, I tried to blast my first serve past Stratton, but the shot was way too long. Instead of hitting my second serve, I stood around feeling lousy about how Stratton'd hammer the next shot back at me.

Banks hollered for me to hurry up, and when I didn't, Allie came over to ask what the delay was.

"Don't you see how he's moved up?" I asked, pointing at Stratton.

"He knows you've got to be careful not to double-fault."

"I won't be able to handle his return."

"Then charge the net."

"That'll make it worse."

"Your charging in might make him overswing."

"What if it doesn't?"

"Let the shot go by. I'll get back and if the ball's in, I'll make the play."

That was a better idea than leaving things to me, so I served and started in toward the net. When Stratton saw that, he squared away to drive the ball straight at me, but before he swung, he saw Allie moving from her side of the court to mine and realized what was going on. He pivoted and hit a forehand into the part of the court Allie was leaving. She had to twist around and lunge at the ball and got off a lob that would've been easy for Stratton or Cabot to play if they'd stayed back. But they'd both come to the net, and the ball was too high to reach and too low to get back and hit. So they turned and watched as the shot landed close enough to the back line you could've said it was in or out depending on where you were at. To me it looked a little long, but the call went to the same kid who'd screwed up earlier, and I figured he'd remember how unpopular his last call'd been and that he'd even things up, but instead he yelled "Out!" again.

The crowd started screaming, and the linesman waited for somebody to give him some protection before trying to split. No one did, though. Banks was looking for the tournament trophy, and Stratton came to the net to get congratulated. I felt as mad as you can get without bursting a blood vessel, and when Stratton held out his hand to get it shaken, I almost smacked him with my racket. But an *F* in PE looks lousy on your report card, so I just walked away.

I figured Allie'd be as upset as I was, but she

went past me up to the net, and after saying a bunch of good-game stuff to Stratton and Cabot, Allie started going around and shaking hands with the judges.

I'd never seen that done before, and neither had the crowd, because they quieted down and watched to see what Allie was going to do when she got to the linesman who'd cost us the tournament. I figured she'd get the guy to put his hand out, and then walk by him like a passing glacier, which would've been a great put-down. But she didn't do that. What she did was shake the linesman's hand in this real friendly way, so it was obvious to everybody she wasn't sore. Then she took off for the locker room.

While Allie was leaving, somebody in the bleachers started clapping. I looked up to see who it was and got a shock because it was my screwball brother. And if his applauding like he'd forgotten how the match'd been stolen wasn't crazy enough, a lot of other people started in too. But I hadn't forgotten, and when Stratton came over in the locker room and tried to give me that good-game stuff, I told him to stuff it, and I wouldn't have cared if he'd gotten physical, because I was really sore.

After school Susan hunted me down to find out when I'd be picking her up that night, but instead of setting a time, I told her that our dating had been a temporary insanity I'd gotten over, and I took off to find my sister.

Liz was going downtown after school to pick up some stuff, and Dad'd told me to go along. When we got going, I mentioned to Liz that I thought Hank was crazy for clapping the way he had.

"What are you talking about?"

"I'm talking about how Hank thought it was great when Allie and I got cheated out of the championship."

Liz didn't say anything until we pulled up to a stoplight, and then she asked if she could explain something to me.

"No," I said.

"Why not?"

"Because you'll go on for an hour about what a good sport Allie was."

"I won't go on for an hour."

"Yes, you will."

"How about if I just talk until we hit another red light?"

I figured I could put up with that, so I agreed, but Liz drove off without taking the Volkswagen out of low gear, and at the speed we were going, she could've talked for an hour just in one block. Actually, I think that's what she meant to do, because she started off by asking if I'd ever noticed the painting of a village at night that Dad has over his desk.

"Do you think I'm blind?" I said.

"Have you noticed it or not?"

"Sure I've noticed it. It's got all those crazy round stars that're as blurry as hell."

"It's by Van Gogh."

"Is that right."

"Have you heard of him?

"No, but do you think this van could go a little faster?"

"What?"

"It's a joke. You know, van like in car and go like in get the hell out of first gear."

"I don't get it."

"Yes, you do."

"No, I don't."

"Yes, you do, but you won't admit it."

"Now I get to talk to you for two red lights," Liz said.

"What?"

"You've taken up my time and you owe me another red light."

"No, I don't."

"It's three red lights if you keep arguing."

Actually, I would've just as soon argued with Liz as heard about her painter, but she wouldn't have put up with that for very long, so I gave her a real bored look while she told me how Van Gogh had only been able to sell one painting his whole life. I thought about mentioning how he should've tried putting things in focus for a change, but I didn't because my sister is taking an art-appreciation course and doesn't want opinions from me.

"Today his paintings sell for millions," Liz said.

"Are you going to get to a point?"

"The point is Van Gogh must've kept painting just because he felt that what he was doing was inspired, and no matter how miserable his life got, he kept seeing this great stuff coming out of his brush."

"That's the point?"

"Yes."

"I don't get it."

"Do you remember the shot Allie made that should've won the tournament?"

"Sure I remember. Do you think I destroy my memory every hour?"

"Did you expect her to try that shot?"

"Nobody did. It was too tough."

"But she took it."

"And it was called out."

"But don't you see how she must've felt when she saw the ball land in?"

"All I know is what it feels like to get cheated."

"That's because you didn't understand what I was saying about Van Gogh."

Liz was going to start up on that painting stuff again, so I told her to pull over to the curb. When she wouldn't, I opened the door and hopped out. We were moving so slow, I thought there'd be no problem getting myself stopped; but I ended up running alongside the Volkswagen until somebody who'd just parked opened their door. When I smacked into it, the guy in the car turned out to be a lot more worried about his door than he was about me, and by the time Liz'd gotten turned around and was coming back, I'd taken off.

I used a city bus to get home, and I had to make so many transfers, I missed dinner.

CHAPTER 14

Saturday morning I was still upset about the tournament, and I figured if I talked to Allie, I might cool down. But when Hank and I got to the Boggses' house, Allie had already left with her mom.

Mr. Boggs was staying home that day, and he poured me a cup of coffee I didn't want and told me Allie was getting her braces off, which she hadn't mentioned to me. Mr. Boggs thought she wanted to surprise me but I doubted that, and I asked him when they'd be home.

He said they'd be gone all day because after the braces were taken care of, Allie and her mom were going to go shopping.

Even though I wasn't that curious, Mr. Boggs explained how he'd just finished a job and had some extra money that he'd talked Allie into using to buy clothes. He also said that because he was between jobs, he had some time to help out in the backyard. I figured we were going to get going as soon as we'd had our coffee, but whenever a little evaporated from my cup, Mr. Boggs poured more in even though I kept telling him that I'd had my fill at home.

Hank'd been luckier than me, because he'd gotten outside before Mr. Boggs decided to drown somebody in coffee, and from where I was sitting, I could see Hank and Emily painting the trim, which was about all that was left to do. The two of them were spending most of their time talking, and if Mr. Boggs didn't jack them up, it was going to be a month before the garage was finished. I could tell, though, that he wasn't going to go outside and act like a foreman, because he was having too great a time talking to me. He was mentioning all sorts of stuff like how Allie never used the family's money to buy clothes, which explained why I'd never seen her wearing the type of outfits you have to go downtown and spend a lot more money on than Allie could make baby-sitting.

Dad used to take Liz shopping downtown when she was younger. That was the sort of thing you'd expect Mom to do, but she felt like a traitor to Gilbert's whenever she bought somewhere else. I'd tag along when Dad took Liz shopping and he and I would sit in the chairs expensive stores have all over the place while Liz modeled clothes. We'd tell Liz which outfits we liked, and I think we had pretty good taste, except, if anything was low-cut or tight, Dad'd tell Liz it made her look fat, which it never did.

That's probably why she goes shopping with her friends now, which is fine, except I miss the way Dad used to take us for ice cream when Liz was done and how every time he'd explain that the stores had chairs so when fathers saw the price of stuff, they'd pass out where they were sitting instead of making a lot of noise falling on the floor. I know that sounds stupid, but it always seemed funny, and so did the model walk Liz'd use while trying on clothes. If we didn't see anyone around, Dad and I would clap in a sophisticated way by using one hand to spank the palm of the other. It's not the sort of clap you'd use at a ball game, but at style shows it's okay because you don't want to make as much noise for a model as you do a ballplayer.

It never bothered me how stupid we acted, but sometimes a sales clerk would come along and give us a look that'd embarrass Dad. If Liz caught the clerk doing that, she'd put back whatever she'd picked out to buy and we'd leave. Usually Liz isn't that sensitive, but she can't stand it when someone acts superior, which is funny considering the women in her boyfriend's family.

Saturday I mentioned to Mr. Boggs that I had a lot of experience in the stores downtown and that Allie should've taken me along. But he said that Allie had pretty good taste, and that when she turned sixteen, she was going to get a job after school so she could afford nicer clothes.

When Mr. Boggs said that, he looked at me like he was wondering why I didn't have a part-time job. He probably figured I got whatever I wanted from my folks, and actually that wasn't it. Working at a hamburger joint is a great way to meet girls, and I would've applied for a job at a place like that a year ago if you didn't have to be so polite to everybody. Even if a customer's rude, you've got to ask them to come back again, and I wouldn't be able to do that. I don't think that makes me lazy, and my boss at the city park was satisfied with the way I worked, except when I ran over stuff or ordered wrong.

When Mr. Boggs finally got going Saturday morning, I kept up with him even though he worked fast and kept doing klutzy stuff the way Allie'd said. He'd bought some bushes he wanted to plant before the first frost. I mentioned to him that it probably wasn't going to freeze that morning even if it was almost October. My saying that didn't make any difference, though, and we dug holes like madmen for half the morning. That's hot work, but whenever we'd want a drink, our water girl was busy whispering with my brother.

I heard them mention the alley a couple times, and I thought Hank might be starting a secret club that'd collect cans for the homeless guys who go through the neighborhood's garbage. But I was wrong about that, because when one of those guys came along, Hank used his regular voice to ask Emily if she had any cans in the house and she said, "Why?"

"I'll take them out to that man in the alley."

"No," Emily said, and you could tell from the way she went ahead and submerged her brush in the paint bucket that she was upset.

I thought she might be confused and figuring the homeless guys were the ones who'd tried to steal tomatoes the week before, so I took a break from digging holes and went over to where Emily and Hank were waiting for the brush in the bucket to bob back up to the top.

"What would those guys do with tomatoes?" I asked Emily. "Make BLTs?"

They looked at me like I was crazy, and before I could explain, Emily took off for the house.

"She doesn't hang around much, does she?" I said to Hank.

"That's what she does when she doesn't like a conversation."

"She's always taking off when I'm around."

"It's probably a coincidence. . . . Do you think that brush is stuck at the bottom of the bucket?"

"I don't think Emily likes me."

"Maybe she doesn't like what you say."

"What's wrong with what I say?"

"Nothing. Emily just might not want to listen to you all the time. . . . Do you think I should reach in and get the brush with my hand?"

"What do the two of you talk about?"

"Stuff."

"What were you whispering about before I came over?"

"If we were whispering, it must've been a secret," Hank said, and when he clams up like that, it isn't any use keeping after him—so I didn't.

Eventually Mr. Boggs and I got the holes dug, and it was when he started planting the bushes that his klutziness really showed up, because he kept sticking the bushes in at crazy angles. At first I tried to tell him we needed to lean the thing right or left, but he'd always overdo it, and I'd end up having to push the bush into position myself; then, before I could get enough dirt in to set it, Mr. Boggs'd angle the bush off again. It wouldn't be until the dirt was in and tamped down that he'd step back and see how crooked things had turned out and we'd have to start over.

That sounds like the sort of thing that'd only happen once, but we must've planted and unplanted each bush three times. By lunch I was having trouble telling what was tilted and what wasn't, so even though Hank hung around to get fed, I split.

CHAPTER 15

Monday morning I wasted so much time finding the shirt I wanted to wear that I missed the bus, and Dad had to give me a ride to school.

Normally, I don't pay much attention to my clothes, but I'd decided that when I talked to Allie about the tournament, I didn't want Hank or Emily or the PE class around. The only way to do that was to go to a movie with her that night. Allie, I mean. We wouldn't be on a date or anything, because I was this older guy who Allie probably saw as a young uncle, and if I ended up paying for everything, it'd only be because I hadn't just gone out and spent all my money on clothes the way Allie had. And if she'd managed to save a little cash, she'd probably end up paying her own way, because she didn't figure to be like Cabot, who expected you to take out a loan before you picked her up.

This favorite shirt I have wasn't in my closet, and after I'd looked under my bed and behind the dresser, Mom told me to check on the clothesline. When Dad heard that, he gave Mom a speech about how whenever the laundry stays out all night, he ends up with moths in his underwear. I don't know if that's true or not, because I've never found any bugs in my stuff, but Dad wears boxer shorts, which is the kind of thing moths might like.

My shirt was on the line and it was dry, but a bird had bombed the front. I scraped at the spot with a clothespin, which made things worse, and I would've just worn a different shirt except the one that'd been stained always got compliments. I wanted to have something pretty sharp on when I asked Allie about going to a movie, so I took the shirt to the bathroom, and while I was scrubbing at the spot, Dad kept sticking his head in to tell me how much later it was getting. Finally he announced, like it was a tragedy, that the bus had left without me. I explained about the shirt, but instead of understanding, Dad had some stuff to say about cleaning bird excrement off in the bathroom sink—I think Dad's the only guy I know who'd bother using a word like *excrement* that early in the morning.

When he was done talking, he handed me some cleanser. I had to scour the whole bathroom practically while my shirt was in the dryer, but I was ready by the time Dad left for work.

I got to school as the first bell was ringing, and on the way in I looked at my shirt to see if it'd picked up any wrinkles. There weren't any, but there also wasn't any color left where I'd scrubbed out the spot, so that the one time I tried to dress nice for school, I ended up looking like I'd been hit by a bleach bullet.

I covered the spot on the way to homeroom by holding an arm across my chest, but that made me look like I was having a spasm, and while Fielding got homeroom going, I tried to figure out what I was going to do about the stain.

Fielding was still reading from the list I told you about, but he kept getting interrupted by wiseguys like Bobby D'Angelo. On Monday D'Angelo waited until Fielding'd read a rule and then stuck his hand into the air.

"Yes?"

"Could you explain that, sir?"

"Explain what?"

"The rule on gum chewing."

"Are you trying to be funny?"

"No, sir."

"The rule says you're not supposed to chew gum, and that's what it means."

"But it doesn't say anything about somebody who just has gum in his pocket."

"What are you talking about?"

"Gum possession, sir. Is it an offense?"

"The rule says nothing about gum possession, young man, and I have no idea why you're making a ruckus over it."

"Am I making a ruckus?"

"You are."

"Just because I want a rule explained?"

"There are other reasons I won't go into because someone else has a question."

"It's not a question, really," a kid named Paul said. "I'd just like to say that you covered ruckus making last week with rule fifteen, and maybe it would help if we reviewed."

"Sixteen," said a girl who sits behind me and never raises her hand when she wants to talk.

"What?" asked Fielding.

"Ruckus making was rule sixteen. I remember because rule fifteen was about making noises, and I know you meant that one for me, and I think it's unfair to give me a rule of my own, because if it was a boy who was cracking his knuckles you wouldn't say a thing."

"Knuckle cracking, young lady, is offensive regardless of sex."

"If we're going into sex," D'Angelo said, "I'll

wait for an answer to my question. But could I ask if sometime this week you could cover gum possession?''

''No.''

''No, it isn't going to be covered, or no, I can't ask?''

''Neither.''

Sometimes I get in on that stuff, because Fielding's asking for it with those rules of his, but I didn't that day because I was busy inking my fingertips and then spitting on them to work up a dye I could use on my shirt. But the ink from the pen turned out way too dark, and I ended up with a dark blue blob in the middle of the bleached-out spot.

After the bell rang, I went into the bathroom and wiped at my shirt with paper towels. That spread the ink to places it hadn't reached on its own, and I would've gone home right then if a guy hadn't walked in wearing a leather jacket. The jacket's that guy's favorite thing, and he wears it to school no matter how hot it is, but by giving him all the money I had except for some change, I got him to rent me the coat for an hour.

I'd wasted too much time in the bathroom to be able to talk to Allie before first period, so I had to wait until after math. When that class got out, I went over to Allie's locker, where there was a swarm of kids, and I wouldn't have even known Allie was in the middle of them except I kept hearing her say thank you to everybody who was telling her how well she'd played in the tournament and how sharp the outfit she had on looked.

Instead of muscling through the crowd to get to Allie, I headed for second-period class, though what I should've done was return the jacket and go home. But I didn't want to do that unless I had to, because the office makes leaving school without a note a pain. They would've had to call Dad, and whenever you phone him at the store about stuff that doesn't have anything to do with hardware, he gets upset and you have to order a pound of nails before he'll talk to you. And I didn't want to have the office call Mom, because whenever an adult gets on the phone and says they're calling in reference to one of her kids, Mom figures there's been a kidnapping and she'll never see me or Hank or Liz again.

I know that's crazy, but once when I was in grade school a kid named Tommie Lagrange talked me into sneaking off campus to a video arcade where it turned out he'd arranged to be kidnapped by his dad. His parents had just finished a custody battle and Tommie wasn't crazy about living with his mom, so he'd cooked up this plan. But Mr. Lagrange couldn't make it to the arcade the way he was supposed to, and instead he'd sent a friend Tommie'd never met. When the guy asked which of us was the Lagrange kid, Tommie panicked and pointed at me.

I told the guy Tommie was lying, but he didn't believe me and an hour later Mr. Lagrange showed up at a motel I'd been checked into and wanted to know who the hell I was. I started crying and didn't stop until Lagrange had taken me back to school. The police were waiting and they called Mom with that we're-phoning-with-reference-to-your-son business that she still worries about.

So rather than have the office call her, it was simpler to split and worry about a note later. But first I wanted to talk to Allie.

After second period I headed for her locker again. This time there were only a couple of people there, so I could've walked right up to her; but I didn't. What I did was stand thirty feet away and stare at what was pretty much a brand new Allie. I won't describe her from top to bottom, because that stuff's boring unless you know the person, but I will mention that her braces were gone, and when she smiled at the people she was talking to, she looked like one of those models on TV game shows who point at prizes—except Allie's smile didn't look plastered on.

I should've figured I'd get spotted if I stood around forever, and when Allie did see me, I got sent an even bigger smile than the one she'd been using on the people by her locker. When I saw that, my breathing got fouled up. I know that sounds stupid, and maybe I was hyperventilating from the heat inside that leather jacket, but I don't think so—there were other guys in the hall besides me who were looking at Allie and gulping for air.

Allie excused herself from the people by her locker and headed my way, but before she got to me, I must've had some sort of brain shutdown because I took off down a side hallway and ended up going out the back door of the school. I even got on the wrong city bus, and when I realized I was heading in the opposite direction from home, I got off without remembering to ask for a transfer. I didn't have enough change left for another ride, so I tried walking home, but I just got more lost, if that's possible.

I finally used the last of my change to call Mom, and when I told her nothing weird was going on and that I was just stranded across town, I could tell she didn't believe me. Even when she found the phone booth I was waiting at, I think she was surprised it was actually me there instead of Tommie Lagrange's dad.

Mom's pretty good about not getting crazy when something besides a kidnapping happens. But when we got home, Dad was waiting in front of the house, and you could tell from the way there was smoke coming from the top of his head that he'd heard about me cutting classes.

"The school must've called him and not ordered any nails," I said.

"I'll talk to him," Mom said while we were getting parked.

"Can't we just drive around until he erupts all over somebody else?" I said, but Mom got out of the car, went over to Dad, and told him to calm down.

"I am calm," Dad said. "I am calm," he repeated, which is what he does when he's out of control. "But I'm not going to condone his cutting classes."

"He may have had a reason."

"I'm not interested in his excuses," Dad said, and I could tell he was getting more worked up all the time, so I got out of the car and walked past my parents into the living room to wait for the lava to flow in behind me, which it did.

Dad can get scary when he's mad, because he stomps around and bangs his fist on everything and keeps asking himself where he went wrong. The whole time he's looking at you like he's trying to decide which wall to shove you through—not that he ever actually gets physical; but when he's denting in furniture, you worry that he'll mistake you for a coffee table and let you have it by accident.

Finally he settled down enough to give me a sermon about skipping school and scaring Mom and a bunch of stuff about being responsible that I wasn't especially interested in, but I acted like I was.

A few hours after that Mom served dinner, which turned out to be a quiet meal. Even Hank didn't have much to say, which surprised me, because usually he tried to smooth things out. But he didn't that night.

I thought the scheme he and Emily'd been whispering about the Saturday before might've gone wrong, so I followed him up to his room and asked if he was in trouble.

"You're the one in trouble, not me," he said.

"Are you mad at me too?" I asked.

"Why would I be?"

"Because I skipped school, I guess."

"Why?"

"Why what?"

"Why did you skip school?"

"My blue shirt got ruined."

"That's all?"

"I was upset about Allie."

Usually Hank's good about asking you stuff so you can explain how you feel, but he didn't seem interested right then, so I asked him if he was okay.

"Emily held my hand on the bus today," he said.

"So?"

"She's never done that before."

"She likes you."

"I guess."

"What else would it be?"

"She didn't hold my hand the way Sally Hopkins did at the Christmas program two years ago."

"Was she the lamb standing next to you in the manger?"

Hank nodded and said, "I asked the teacher not to put Sally next to me, but she said a boy lamb has to stand next to a girl lamb. So every time a wise man or a shepherd got in front of us, Sally'd grab my hand, and when they uncovered the baby Jesus, Sally kissed me."

"Maybe Emily's just getting ready to kiss you."

"I don't think so."

"Why not?"

"Because she didn't hold my hand the way Sally did."

"How did Emily hold your hand?"

"Like I held on to Liz's when she was teaching me to swim in the deep end of the pool."

"You're imagining things. Emily's just a hard hand-holder."

"You think so?"

"Absolutely."

"Do you think I should talk to Liz?"

"Didn't we just settle it?"

"I guess so."

"So let's drop it. Do you want to hear what happened to me today?"

"Okay."

"Did I tell you I was going to ask Allie to a movie?"

"You never tell me about your dating."

"This wasn't going to be a date. It was just me and Allie going to a movie."

"What did she say?"

"I didn't ask her."

"Why not?"

"A bird crapped on my shirt."

"Allie wouldn't have cared about that."

"Maybe not, but I did."

"Were you worried she'd say no?"

"Why would she say no?" I asked, and I raised my voice a little, because the idea of Allie turning me down seemed a little crazy.

"I guess she wouldn't have," said Hank.

"Did she say something on the bus ride home about me?"

"I sat with Emily."

"But you talked to Allie, didn't you?"

"We said hello."

"Is that all?"

"I told her I liked her dress."

"You didn't talk about me?"

"Why would we talk about you?"

"I don't know. Maybe she wanted to tell you what a jerk I was at school."

"Liz tells me that stuff."

"So you and Allie just talked about her dress?"

"And about her hair."

"What about her hair?"

"She got it cut."

"I didn't notice that."

"It looks nice."

"She's different, isn't she?" I asked.

"What do you mean?"

"I mean with the braces gone and the new clothes and everything, she's like a new Allie."

"She's the same."

"I know she's the same person, but she looks better now."

"She always looked good."

"Not like she does now."

"To me she did."

"Are you talking about her hair and teeth and stuff?"

"Not really," Hank said, and you could tell he wanted to mention things about Allie that were too subtle for me to have noticed, which I didn't want to hear, so I went over to Hank's window and stared outside for a while with my back to him. You can't do that to most people, but it's okay with Hank, and he didn't try to throw me out of his room, which I appreciated because I was trying to figure out if I was like those idiots who'd been ignoring Allie last Friday, but who were all over her at school on Monday.

I mean, I hate it when somebody is treated a certain way just because of their clothes or how athletic they are—not that I get snubbed by anybody on account of that stuff. Dad owning a hardware store makes everybody think my family's got a lot of money, and I don't know if we do or not, because I don't care enough to ask. What I do is treat people rotten or not depending on what I think of them and not by how much money their parents have.

But Allie didn't know that, and she might've figured I was just asking her out because she'd gotten popular, and it wasn't like that.

When I turned back to Hank and explained what I'd been thinking, he said, "Allie wouldn't have cared why you wanted a date."

"I told you, it wasn't a date. We were just going to go to a movie the way you would with Emily."

"Emily and I don't date."

"Neither do Allie and I."

"Why not?"

"Why would I want to date somebody as young as her?"

"She's not that young."

"She always seemed more your age than mine."

"She didn't look my age on the bus today."

"I know," I said.

"So why didn't you ask her out?"

"I don't know."

"Didn't you think you'd have any fun?"

"Why wouldn't we have fun?"

"I don't know."

"We have fun Saturday mornings, don't we?"

"It'd be different."

"Why?" I asked.

"You said Allie was different."

"But better. She looked better than Cabot even."

"Do you like Cabot?" Hank asked, and I hate it when he jumps around from one subject to another.

"Why wouldn't I like her?"

"What do you talk about?"

"What difference does it make?"

"I don't know. I'm just curious what you say to each other."

"Do you think I write everything down?"

"What do you say when you first pick Cabot up?"

"The first thing?"

"Yes."

"I ask her if I have to go in and talk to her dad."

"What do you say when you're on the way to the movie?"

"Usually I tell her I like her outfit, and she tells me where she got it."

"What about after the movie?"

"She tells me how she's had a lot of the same experiences we saw people having in the film—which is funny, considering the shows we see."

"Do you talk about other stuff?"

"Not a lot. She's pretty self-centered when you think about it. But all the girls I go out with are that way."

"Why do you go out with them?"

"You mean besides the way they look?"

"Yes."

"I suppose I feel good going out with someone that's popular. But that's connected to the way they look, isn't it?"

"A little."

"I like it that there's never any long silences. Girls like Cabot are always telling you where they're going over Christmas or what schools have accepted them to college."

"Would Allie do that?"

"Sophomores don't apply to colleges," I said. Hank didn't say anything back, which is usually what he does if you get his point but are pretending that you don't. Finally I said, "She wouldn't brag like Susan, if that's what you mean."

"Oh," said Hank.

"Are you getting at something or what?"

"I suppose."

"Then let's change the subject," I said.

"Can I ask something about you and Allie first?"

"What?"

"Have you held her hand?"

"Are you still worrying about that thing with Emily?"

"Yes."

"Well, don't. She thinks you're cute, that's all."

"Okay."

I know I should've let Hank talk about Emily, but I didn't. I just split.

CHAPTER 16

The next day, before I could get into my classes, I had to go see Mr. Iverson, who's a vice-principal that must've been a minister once, the way he preaches. After a while I thought he was going to go ahead and baptize me, but before he got to that, his secretary showed up and told him there were five kids in the waiting room who'd been caught smoking pot on the roof. You could tell that getting high was about the worst thing Iverson thought you could do, and he wrote my admission pass so fast, you could hardly read it.

When I got out into the waiting room, I saw that one of the pot smokers was the guy I'd rented the jacket from. I said hello and everything, but all he was interested in was where his jacket was. I told him that if he could stick around after he was done getting suspended, I would grab the jacket out of my locker before second period class.

He said that he and his friends would like it better if I just gave him the combination to my locker. Normally that's something you don't want to do, but they were a big group to disappoint, so I gave them the numbers and headed for class.

Right at the end of first period Iverson showed up in math and asked me to step out of the room. When I got out into the hall, I saw that there were pens and pencils and tablets spread around everywhere. At first I thought somebody'd set off some kind of silent bomb in the school store that sells supplies, but then I saw how there was a lot of personal stuff lying around that'd all come from my locker. And just when I was wishing I hadn't given my combination out, Iverson asked me what my problem was.

"You think I did this?"

"Your name's all over everything."

"I'd have to be crazy to do this to my own stuff."

"I agree," Iverson said, and he hauled me off to the school psychologist's office. Usually you don't get sent there unless you're acting really weird, and the first chance I got, I explained how I'd given my combination away to some guys who were mad at me because I'd taken off the day before with a jacket I was wearing to cover up some crap on my shirt. But the psychologist wasn't interested. What he was interested in was giving me a million tests, so that by the time I got out of there, the bell for lunch had rung.

Instead of going to the cafeteria, where Allie was probably being crowned queen of the school, I grabbed a Coke at the store that's run by the student council and went outside to hang around on the front steps of the school with some other guys.

That's where I was when my sister showed up. She said she wanted to talk to me, and if I could've told her we'd talk later I would've, but with Liz you don't get a choice.

We went over to a statue that's on the school's front lawn, and rather than the how's-your-day stuff most people use to get a conversation going, Liz asked me why I'd been avoiding Allie.

"Who says I'm avoiding her?"

"She does."

"Maybe she's wrong."

"Maybe you better give me a straight answer."
Liz wasn't going to put up with me fooling around, so I told her that I didn't feel like joining the crowd of worshipers that were hanging around Allie.

"Do you think she wants all of that attention?"

"If she didn't, she'd tell them to get lost."

"Not everybody is as rude as you."

"If Allie had any sense, she'd know they're just being nice because she looks better than she used to and that they're all too dumb to know she hasn't really changed."

"Have you been talking to Hank?"

"What's he got to do with anything?"

"You sounded like him just now."

"Can't I have a sensitive idea without you thinking I got it from him?"

"No," Liz said as she looked up at a pigeon that was coming in to land on one of the statue's heads. It had two. One was on a horse, and the other belonged to a soldier who was standing up in stone stirrups. Standing up isn't the best thing for a soldier that's out in front of a high school to do, because underclassmen are always sneaking onto campus at night with a bag of underwear or their mother's old prom dress so that at least once a week a janitor has to go out and undress the general, which is what everybody calls the guy on the horse. He used to have a stone hat, but somebody chiseled that off, and when the pigeon Liz was watching landed, it ended up on the general's scalp or whatever it is statues have after their hat's been stolen.

Liz smiled at the bird like she was welcoming it to our conversation—which made me mad because it was the sort of thing Hank would've done if he'd been there. It was like the two of them belonged to a club I couldn't join, and when Liz looked back at me, I asked her why she didn't mind her own business. I expected to get decked for that, but instead she walked off, which was fine because until Allie didn't show up for PE, I couldn't see why we had to get together before seventh period. It wasn't until that last hour that I found out Allie'd joined the swim team, and even though I shouldn't have been surprised, I was, and kind of upset.

After school I got on the bus and walked by where Allie was sitting without saying hello, and when she came back and sat down next to me, I ignored her.

Allie didn't try to talk to me, and I finally mentioned I liked what she was wearing, which I more or less had to do because she had on a great-looking jean skirt outfit, and if I hadn't said something, it would've been like I was going blind.

She thanked me and smiled, and I know you're going to think I'm lying, but I started having trouble breathing again. I wasn't able to talk for a minute, which gave Allie a chance to explain how she'd tried all day to let me know she was dropping PE. She even had an explanation about why she'd joined the swim team, but I didn't catch it. I was noticing how she didn't have much makeup on, and I kept wanting to touch her face, but I knew that would've been crazy, so I didn't.

"Richard?" Allie said after she was done explaining about PE.

"What?"

"Did you listen to what I was telling you?"

"Pretty much."

"And you're not mad?"

"Not really."

"You haven't said much."

"Is that right?"

"Are you upset I wasn't home last Saturday?"

"Why would I be upset about that?"

"I thought maybe you got bored working with Dad."

"He was okay."

"Did he tell you any dumb stuff?"

"Like what?"

"I don't know—father stuff."

"You mean dirty jokes?"

"No. Sometimes if I'm not around to stop him, Dad starts bragging about Emily and me."

"We were too busy tilting bushes for him to do much bragging."

"So you didn't mind my not being there?"

"You don't need my permission to go shopping."

"I know. But I thought maybe that's why you were mad."

"Why do you keep saying I'm mad?" I was getting irritated with all of Allie's questions, so I said, "If you want to drop out of PE a month before the swim season starts, that's okay with me."

"I explained that the coach is putting us on a conditioning program."

"Fine."

"Didn't Susan tell you that?"

"I haven't seen her since Friday."

"Are you mad about the tournament?" Allie asked, sort of changing the subject, which for once I didn't mind.

"I didn't like getting cheated, if that's what you mean."

"We played our best match Friday."

"So?"

"So nothing, Richard. We played well, that's all."

"It impressed the hell out of your new friends."

"Is there something wrong with people liking the way we played?"

"We?"

"You won the second set for us."

"So?"

"So there's no reason to be jealous."

"Do you think I care what anyone thinks of the way I played?" I said, and I must've been raising my voice, because some kids in the front of the bus turned around to see what was going on.

"I don't know if you care or not," Allie said.

"I don't. Not at all."

"Then I'm sorry," said Allie, and I probably should've accepted her apology, but I didn't. What I did instead was stand up and ask Allie to let me out of my seat.

"We're still five blocks from your house," she said.

"I'm not waiting until the last second to get ready to get off the bus the way I usually do."

"Can we talk on the way to school tomorrow?"

"I'm going to be catching a ride with Liz from now on."

"Will you be over this weekend?"

"No."

Allie swung around so I could get out, and I didn't say good-bye or mention that the reason I wouldn't be over Saturday was that I'd gotten stuck with three weeks of Saturday detention for getting my locker destroyed, which I thought was just as much a joke as Allie thinking I was jealous. In fact, if she was going to think stuff like that, I didn't see any reason the two of us should bother seeing each other. Not that we would much anyway, because with her out of PE and me not going over Saturdays, the only time we'd meet would be on the bus.

I figured I could avoid even that if I could catch a ride the rest of the year with my sister—Liz'd bought an old Chrysler that had a lot of stuff they used to put on cars to make them weigh a million pounds. The car was such an embarrassment that when she'd brought the thing home the week before, I'd told Liz to park it in the back, and she didn't forget me saying that because when I told her how I wanted to ride to school with her the rest of the year, she asked me if I was going to hide on the floorboards so no one would see me in her car.

"Did you think I was serious about that back-yard thing? That was a joke. I know a classic automobile when I see one."

"Why do you want a ride?"

"You're graduating this year. We should spend time together."

"Why do you want a ride?"

"It's a personal thing, okay? I'll give you five bucks a week for gas if you don't ask me any questions."

"That's not enough."

"Five a week will get even that dinosaur of yours back and forth to school. You don't expect me to pay for the rest of your riding around, too, do you?"

"I want you to find out what Hank's up to."

"What are you talking about?" I said, and instead of answering me, Liz had me follow her from the living room to the kitchen, where even though Hank had just gotten home, he was already on the phone to Emily. I know it was her because he'd said her name when we walked into the kitchen. Once he saw we were there, he waited a couple of seconds to see if we were going to leave, and when we didn't, he told Emily he'd call right back and headed for another phone. That sort of thing is unusual for him, because he's real open about stuff.

"Do you know what he's up to?" Liz asked when Hank was gone.

"You're the one he talks to all the time," I said.

"He's planning something with Emily and he won't tell me what it is."

"If I find out what's going on, can I get a ride to school?"

"If it's something crazy and you stop him."

I was going to shake hands with Liz to set the deal, but I think she felt guilty about arranging to have one brother spy on another, so she just left the room without saying anything else. She did look at the phone in a pretty meaningful way on the way out, though, so I went over and picked it up. Hank was on an extension, and because I was alone, I didn't bother covering up the mouthpiece. That turned out to be a mistake, because Dad came in the back door and asked in a just-been-outside-mowing-lawn voice who I was talking to.

"Nobody," I said and then, when it was too late, I covered up the mouthpiece.

"Richard?" Hank said from the phone upstairs.

"If you're not talking to anyone," Dad asked, "why are you covering up the mouthpiece?"

"I don't know," I said, and took my hand away.

"What are you doing on the line?" Hank asked.

"I don't know," I said to Hank.

"I heard you the first time," Dad said, and went over to wash his hands.

"What did you overhear?" Hank asked me.

"Nothing," I said, and I tried to keep my voice down so Dad wouldn't hear.

But even with the water running he did and said, "Nothing?"

"That's right," I said.

"Then get off the line," said Hank.

"Me?" Emily asked.

"Nothing what?" asked Dad.

"Richard, not you, Emily," said Hank.

"Nothing, nothing, Dad."

"Has Richard been listening in long?" asked Emily.

"I wasn't," I said.

"You weren't?" asked Dad.

"That's right," I said.

"You weren't what?" Dad said in a voice loud enough for Emily and Hank to hear.

"Is your father listening in too?" Emily asked Hank.

"If you don't get off this line, Richard, I'm going to tell Dad how the car got that scratch along the side."

Hank was talking about a couple weeks before when he and I'd gone to the mall and passed a couple of girls who were sitting on the hood of a parked car. One of them had smiled at me, or maybe at the Lincoln, but either way I came around and when I was passing them again, I steered close to their car. What I'd meant to do was come within an inch to show them what a daredevil driver I was. Instead what happened was that I scraped the Lincoln against the fender of the car the girls were on. The only damage, besides knocking the girls off the hood of their car, was a gash that got put on the passenger side of the Lincoln. When I saw it, I decided to kill myself. But Hank wouldn't drive the car over me the way I wanted, so I told him he'd have to back me up if I lied to Dad about the car—which is what I ended up doing. Hank never mentioned anything about where the scratch had come from until the threat he made. That got me so worried, I told him again a lot louder than I should've that I hadn't heard a thing he'd said.

"That's because," Dad said, "I didn't speak."

"Get off the line," said Hank.

"Okay," said Emily.

"Emily?" said Hank.

"I think I'll call later," I told Dad, and put the phone down.

"Who were you going to call?"

"Nobody," I said.

"Let me guess what you were going to talk about."

"What?"

"Nothing," Dad said, and laughed like he'd made a joke. I didn't get it, which wasn't surprising because I don't understand half of what Dad says.

I went upstairs, and when Hank showed up I tried to tell him that I'd been doing research for a report on telephone speech patterns, but he didn't believe that for a second. He jumped me and gave the inside of my right leg a wicked pinch.

I should've stopped snooping after that, but instead I waited until Hank'd gone downstairs and went into his room. I thought there might be some letters lying around from Emily, and I was in the middle of going through a dresser when Hank walked in. I figured I'd get a speech about what a disappointment I was as a brother, but instead he went right for the spot on my leg he'd pinched before, and I was pretty interested in keeping him away from there.

I could've hit Hank over the head with a lamp, but if I had and Liz'd found out, I'd have been riding the bus forever. So I held Hank out away from me while I worked toward the doorway. When I got there, I gave Hank a shove which he must've been waiting for because he went limp, and my shove had nothing to go against. I tumbled back into the room and Hank was able to attach his hand to my leg before I could get another hold on him. Instead of pinching, he asked if I was going to spy on him anymore. I said I wasn't, but he went ahead and pinched me anyway, and if you could lose a leg from that sort of thing, I would've lost mine.

CHAPTER 17

The next day Liz gave me a ride to school so she could get a progress report.

"You didn't find out *anything*?" she asked when I told her what'd happened.

"I found out Hank's a great pincher."

"You don't know what you're doing, do you?"

"I'm just getting started."

"Why don't you read up on detecting?"

"I haven't seen any books around about spying on your brother."

"I'll let you look at the Sherlock Holmes story we're reading in lit class."

"That guy was a hundred years ago."

"I'm halfway through the story and he hasn't gotten pinched yet."

"Is he following a nine-year-old boy?"

"A hound."

"Then he's more likely to get bitten, isn't he?"

"Maybe you'd better give up."

"Do I still get to ride with you?"

"No."

"Then I'll keep trying."

"Hank's going to be careful when he's around you."

"When he's with Emily, he'll forget about me."

"When do you see them together?"

"They ride the bus together."

"And you're with me."

"They talk all Saturday morning."

"You've got detention."

"I could have someone else watch them. Allie could do it."

"Are you and Allie talking to each other again?"

"We were for a little while yesterday."

"Are you still?"

"Probably not."

"Then I'm driving you to school for nothing."

I'd had enough criticism for one ride, so I told Liz to pull the car over and let me out.

"We're only a block from school," she said.

"Then pull over."

"This is practically where I park."

"So park."

I thought about slamming the door when I got out, but I didn't figure I'd get away with that, so I settled for not walking Liz the rest of the way to school, which I'm sure broke her heart. At least I'd given her the idea that she couldn't hassle me every morning about what I'd found out, which was a good thing because information turned out to be hard to get. In fact, I probably would've given up, except I knew Liz was right to be worried about what Hank was up to.

Once when Hank was six, he tunneled under our neighbor's lawn, and even though the tunnel was over ten feet long, the opening into it was so small, Hank convinced Dad it was just a cave for storing stuff Mom wouldn't let into the house. But storage was just what Hank intended to do with the hole after he was done using it as a mine shaft.

Hank'd gone to a program at the public library where they'd talked about the mining history of Montana and how most people don't own the mineral rights to whatever is beneath their property. I don't think Hank understood most of what was said, but when he got home he went into the backyard and started digging. A couple feet down he found a vein of what must've been coal, which in little amounts isn't worth anything, but Hank got excited anyway.

As he dug, the vein angled off toward our neighbor's yard, so Hank went next door to offer Mr. Collins half of everything.

Collins had just put a swimming pool in, and I don't think he would've let anyone tear up his backyard, but there was no way he was even going to consider anything Hank had to say. Collins had a rotten habit of shooting at cats that came on his property and whenever my brother'd catch him doing that, he'd call the cops. Usually they wouldn't even come out, because they didn't intend to do anything with a complaint turned in by a kid. But Collins was upset about being reported, and when Hank was finished explaining as much as he could remember about mineral rights, Collins slammed the door in my brother's face.

That's when Hank decided to dig a tunnel. He didn't know enough to do it himself, so he got a friend named Eugene, whose dad is an engineer, to help him. Usually Eugene built stuff like the rocket he'd used to launch his dog over the roof of their house, so my folks should've watched what was going on in the backyard more closely, but they didn't, not even when Hank and Eugene hauled more dirt to the garden than you'd get out of a dozen storage caves.

Ten feet into the digging Eugene went on vacation with his family, and before Hank reached the eleven-foot mark, he came up against Collins's swimming pool. He didn't know that, though. He just thought he'd hit an incredibly flat rock that was going to have to be blasted out of the way.

Hank emptied the powder from firecrackers Dad'd bought for the Fourth of July into a bag and laid it against the part of Collins's swimming pool that the digging had uncovered. Then he hooked up some string to the bag and lit it from outside the tunnel. The whole thing worked pretty well, except instead of the explosion Hank expected there was mostly fizzing like he'd filled up his tunnel with Alka-Seltzer and water; there was enough of a bang, though, to collapse the ground that'd been on top of the tunnel.

Collins was cleaning his pool when part of his property caved in, and all the smoke coming from our side of the fence made him think geologic activity was taking place, and the guy immediately started draining his pool so there'd be less pressure on the walls.

When Collins found out what'd really happened, he tried to get Dad to pay for the water that'd been wasted. Dad didn't mind coming over and fixing Collins's yard, but he thought emptying a pool to take pressure off the walls had been stupid, and he told Collins that. Dad also told Collins that he should have more of a sense of humor about what'd happened, but Dad was just saying that. Everybody in our family was sore at Hank for queering our chances at going to pool parties, and even Liz gave him a lecture about not doing dangerous stuff. But she must've been worried that her speech had worn off, because she was pretty anxious for me to find out what was going on.

Unfortunately, I wasn't much of a detective, and I ended up lying around Hank's room whenever I could and bugging him to tell me what he was up to. Most of the time I think he wanted to throw me out, but he probably felt sorry for me because of what'd happened with the tennis tournament, and Allie, and my Saturdays—when Dad found out about me getting detention hall, he cut me off from the Lincoln, which was kind of like getting a punishment for getting a punishment. I thought that was stupid, but I didn't say anything, because the only time I really wanted his car was when I was going on a date, which for some reason I'd lost interest in. And if you're not taking girls out, a Volkswagen's just as good to drive around in as a Lincoln.

The Saturday of the second weekend in October was my last day of detention and my folks'd set up a barbecue with the Boggses to celebrate their garage finally getting painted. If the thing'd been planned for a weeknight I would've skipped it, because I'd been avoiding Allie for three weeks, and I didn't want to run into her in my own backyard.

But on Saturday night I was sure she'd be dated up because I'd heard guys had been asking her out like mad. I guess she'd turned them all down at first but had finally gone out with a guy on the swim team. According to somebody who knew the guy, Allie's date turned into an octopus halfway through the movie they went to, and Allie'd just about knocked him out with a giant box of Milk Duds. But one date like that wasn't going to discourage her forever, and I figured there was no chance she'd come to something as corny as a family barbecue—which was okay with me, because it'd be easier to concentrate on watching Hank and Emily if Allie wasn't around.

But I wasn't any better at predicting than I was at detecting, because Allie did show up. She said hello to me, and I said hello back, but my timing was off and my hello didn't come out until Allie'd walked off, so that I looked like I was talking to some invisible guy. For a while that invisible guy was the only company I had, because Allie was talking to Liz, and Hank was with Emily, and all four parents were lying around the lawn furniture drinking beer. The only thing more ignored than me was the food on the grill. When the smoke from there got thick, Dad went over and lifted the hood. The rush of air made the steaks catch fire, and while the adults and Allie and

Liz ran over to try to put the fires out, Hank went into the house.

And he didn't go in through the back door the way you'd expect—he went around to the front of the house. I don't think he planned on anybody noticing he was gone, because it'd gotten dark enough so that the only real light was from the bulbs Dad'd hooked up on the deck. Hank'd probably expected everyone to run over to the grill, but I'd been watching Dad torch steaks my whole life, and Mom and Liz were only acting interested to be polite. Hank had allowed for that, though, by having Emily go stand by the back door. If anyone had tried to go into the house, I'm sure Emily would've delayed them somehow. When I heard the kitchen phone ringing, I thought about testing her out, but Hank must've been waiting for the call because he answered right away, and I knew it was too late to affect whatever it was he was doing.

While the steaks burned themselves out and everyone was busy examining the remains, I poured my Coke into the grass and filled the can with the beer Mom had left behind when she'd run over to the grill. I had half the can gone by the time Hank finally came outside, and I gave him a wink like I was in on his scheming. He didn't wink back.

"I must've spilled my beer," Mom said as she sat back down in her lawn chair and picked up her can.

"Richard's probably been pouring it into his Coke can again," Liz said, and before I could call her a liar, cops started coming through the back gate.

At first I thought the police were making the quickest arrest in the history of underage drinking, but nobody seized my Coke can or even seemed interested in me. The police wanted to talk to Mr. Boggs, and then Hank. Not much of what I heard made sense, especially after parents of kids in Hank's grade showed up in our yard and started to shout about grapes.

When everybody'd left and Hank'd been quarantined in his room, I snuck in to talk to him. At first Hank didn't have anything to say, so we sat in the dark without talking until he asked if I remembered the Saturday morning I'd chased the tomato raiders out of the Boggses' yard.

When I told him I did, he said, "While you were running them off, Emily was looking to see who they were. The next school day she walked up to one of them on the playground and punched him in the face. She didn't knock him down or anything, but he was sore anyway and was getting ready to hit Emily back when I showed up and threatened to call a teacher over. That didn't worry him, because he said he was the one who'd gotten hit first. When Emily said she'd turn him in for raiding gardens, he laughed and said that Emily could go ahead and tell anyone she wanted, because they weren't going to do anything to someone his age for stealing a few vegetables."

"What did Emily think about the kid laughing at her?"

"She tried to take another poke at him. I hauled her off, but I figured I had to think of a way to get the garden raiding stopped or Emily'd end up doing something crazy."

"So you poisoned the Boggses' grapes?"

"We pretended to poison them and painted a sign that had a fake warning on it. Then during lunch yesterday Emily and I sat so we'd be overheard talking about how all the Boggses were coming over for a barbecue Saturday."

"Didn't you think the raiders'd see the sign before they ate any grapes?"

"I knew it'd be pretty dark by the time they got there, and we made the sign small so nobody'd notice it until they'd gone along the vines."

"And they fell for that?"

"For what?"

"For a sign?"

"It was probably more the dead birds Emily put under the vines."

"Where'd she get dead birds?"

"I followed Evan Clark around while he was shooting sparrows with his BB gun."

"And you picked up what he shot?"

"It made me feel kind of sad."

"I bet."

"When I had enough birds, I told Evan you'd bust his gun if he ever shot anything in our alley again."

"I never said that."

"I know."

"Even if I cared enough about sparrows to think it, I wouldn't say anything. Clark's older brother is an all-city wrestler."

"Evan told me that, but I said you wouldn't care."

I couldn't see Hank's face to tell if he was proud of putting five kids in the hospital, but his voice didn't sound like he was happy about what'd happened. "I was still worried that if the raiders waited too long to break in, the timing of the phone calls would be off."

"What phone calls?"

"The ones that got made when the raiders started showing up at their homes saying they'd been poisoned. I'd figured things so that if the grapes got eaten around six, the parents would be calling our house to talk to Mr. Boggs while Dad was setting fire to dinner. When it happened that way, I was able to come in and take the calls without anyone else answering the phone."

"Why would those parents put up with talking to you instead of Mr. Boggs?"

"I told them that the Boggses hadn't gotten to our house yet because they'd met Dad down at his store to pick up some bird poison. I mentioned a poison's name I'd looked up that has to be pumped out of any stomachs it gets into. A couple parents wanted to know how I remembered what the poison was called. I told them that Dad'd written the name on a pad by the phone when Mr. Boggs'd called up to order it."

"Did you figure on the cops getting involved?"

"I did, but I didn't think they'd notice the BB holes in the birds, and they must not've, because the word got given for the pumping to start."

"I had that done to me once when I was a kid," I said.

"You told me about it."

"It was awful."

"That's what you said."

When the cops'd shown up at the barbecue, Hank'd tried to explain what he'd done, but nobody listened until he pretty much yelled at them. He didn't mention what Emily'd done, but she did, and that gave the cops two kids to holler at. Dad had a bunch of stuff to say, too, but nothing seemed to bother Hank as much as the way Mom was standing around looking disappointed.

I don't know what bothered Emily, because when the yelling got bad, Allie hauled her off. One of the cops tried to stop them, but Allie pushed by and Mr. Boggs said to let them go because he was responsible for Emily's actions—which I thought was dumb, because Emily had to stop getting protected sometime. I didn't say anything, though, because there were enough people giving their opinions already.

When the cops got around to asking Hank why he'd come up with such a crazy plan, he told them how there were older people getting their gardens ruined and that nothing was being done about it. After Hank'd said that, the cops were a little less anxious to hang around, and once they'd explained what charges were going to be filed, they took off.

It was right after that that the parents of the garden raiders started showing up. You could tell they were sore at Hank, so Mom went ahead and took him inside. Though if she was worried that somebody was going to smack him, she shouldn't have been. Dad got pretty protective and told all the parents who were coming into the yard that if they hadn't raised such juvenile delinquents, Hank wouldn't have had to pretend he'd poisoned anybody. At first the parents claimed their kids hadn't been doing anything wrong, but when Mr. Boggs asked them how their kids had gotten a bellyful of his grapes, the parents shut up a little.

They didn't make any trouble at the hearing, either, a week later, where a judge named Talbot said that all seven kids involved had shown a reckless disregard for the community. You could tell the kids were wondering if that was good or bad, but the cops didn't have any trouble getting the message when the judge bawled them out for not being more vigilant in protecting homeowners from nuisances which might seem minor to the police, but which, to the elderly, would be perceived as a significant problem. That's pretty much exactly as the judge put it, and I think she must've had a dictionary in front of her the whole time.

I was starting to think that Talbot was like Dad and made you wait a year to find out what the punishment was going to be. But finally she got around to saying how her concern for the elderly was especially pertinent during October because the property rights of the elderly were under special assault at Halloween.

"Therefore," the judge said, "as a means of expressing a sensitivity to the importance of the older citizens in our community, I'm ordering that on the night before Halloween the seven children involved in this incident, and as many members of the police force as can be spared from duty, will present an amateur night in the police-station meeting room for the entertainment of senior citizens and for the education of the adults in our community, and through us our children."

Listening to that speech just about exhausted me, and I would've stopped paying attention right at the start if I hadn't thought the judge was going crazy right there in front of everybody. But nobody in the courtroom except Emily and me seemed to think the judge's plan was nuts. And from the way Emily's head disappeared inside the collar of the dress she had on, it was obvious performing in public wasn't something she was crazy about.

I asked Hank later why that was, and he said Mrs. Boggs'd told him that when Emily was younger she'd had a piano teacher who'd figured Emily for a prodigy. This guy'd set up a recital that went well at first, but then somebody came in late and made a lot of noise getting to their seat. People turned around to see what was happening, which isn't that unusual. Even on the classical station Mom and Dad listen to, you can hear guys coughing and blowing their noses in the background all the time. Musicians probably have to get used to that sort of thing from the audience, but nobody'd told Emily that.

She stopped playing and when her teacher came onstage to find out what the holdup was, Emily said she wanted to do a different piece. The teacher wasn't happy, but Emily wouldn't continue otherwise, so she got the okay. By then the audience was wondering what was up, and when Emily started in on something that wasn't on the program, everybody started whispering, so that Emily stopped playing and started to cry.

I guess she hasn't played for anybody outside her family, or cried, since.

You could tell Hank felt bad about having thought up something that ended with Emily in a spot, but bad as he felt, I think Emily felt worse.

CHAPTER 18

Dad was plenty upset by the fake poisoning, but he'd cooled down by the time Hank had his police-station act ready to show the family, and we sat around the living room while Hank told jokes that you had to be nine years old to appreciate, like "How do you catch a unique rabbit?" When nobody knew, Hank said, "Unique up on it." That cracked him up, but what really got to him was the next line: "Then how do you catch a tame rabbit?" Hank looked around at us for a couple seconds and then said, "The tame way."

I thought Hank was going to hurt himself the way he laughed over that, and it was pretty much the same for every one he told; in fact, by the middle of each joke he was so out of control that when he finally delivered a punch line, he had to take an intermission, he was so exhausted.

For a while everybody just sat and watched. But then the whole thing started to seem silly, and by the time Hank was done with his routine, we were laughing as hard as he was. Later I told him not to count on the audience at the police station laughing like his own family had, but that didn't bother Hank. He figured the jokes were funny, and it was okay with him if nobody else did—which was lucky, because I figured those senior citizens were going to be a tough crowd.

I think Emily agreed with me about that, because when she came over to our house for a rehearsal, she kept her funeral face on through all of Hank's act even though the five garden raiders were getting ready to wet their pants, they were laughing so hard.

When Hank was done, the raiders got themselves arranged in the middle of the living room and took a bow. Hank and I applauded while Emily sat there like she was wishing they'd all drop dead. When one of them stepped forward and took another bow, Hank and I clapped again, and the kid introduced him and his buddies as "The Great Saltinis." I thought he'd meant to say "Santinis," because that seems to be a popular name for circus acts. But when they got going, you could see the kid had given the right name, because he opened up a package of saltine crackers and passed them out to his partners. On a signal from the guy who'd opened the package, crackers started getting tossed around like mad, and it was neat, because no saltines that I saw got dropped or accidentally tossed into the kitchen.

When the juggling part of the act was over, Hank and I applauded while the Saltinis passed out the crackers they'd been using. I suppose I should've eaten a couple to be polite, but I didn't, because kids that age never wash their hands. I just set my crackers on a table while Hank ate his and Emily crushed hers.

The Saltinis announced that the next part of their act was supposed to be a human pyramid, but because the ceiling in our living room was so low, a human rectangle was going to be done instead; and even though they didn't have any problems doing the stunt, you could tell they were disappointed in how it had looked.

While Hank made a big deal of how he could imagine what the pyramid would've looked like, the Saltinis got ready for their last stunt by hauling a plank into the house. They propped the thing up on two concrete blocks, and Hank asked them if the audience wouldn't be a little disappointed to see somebody balancing across such a wide board. Emily piped up for the first time to say that if there wasn't any chance of them breaking their necks, nobody'd be interested in watching. The head Saltini said that they were going to set the board up so nobody'd be able to see how wide it was. Then they were going to lay people's watches underneath the board, where they'd be destroyed if anything went wrong.

They wanted to use my watch but I refused. Hank ended up getting a wall clock from the kitchen, and when everything was in place, three of the Saltinis mounted the board on one end and two on the other. They wobbled toward the middle, where they pushed and shoved past each other. I thought the wall clock was history, but they managed to get by each other without falling. They said later that they'd been faking their shakiness, but Hank suggested that for the show they only get watches from people they knew. He also told them that they should try to get a board that didn't have so many knots in it, but you could tell they thought my brother was getting paranoid.

After the Saltinis had cleared their stuff away, Hank got up and gave Emily an introduction she pretty much ignored. Even after Hank pointed at the piano we have in the living room, Emily stayed stuck to the couch. Finally Hank walked over to her and said, "It's time, Emily."

"Everyone's still here."

"We're your audience."

"You have to leave."

"The show's only a week away. Don't you want to practice in front of people?"

"No."

"How about for me?" asked Hank.

"Everyone else will leave?"

"They can wait in the kitchen."

"In the backyard."

"Will you take everyone outside?" Hank asked me.

"Seriously?"

"Yes."

I was going to ask if I had to drag the audience out the night of the show, too, but Hank gave me a look, so I kept my mouth shut and led the Saltinis to the backyard, where they cooked up a plan to set off a fire alarm right after Emily was introduced at the police station. They figured that'd let her play while everybody was outside waiting for the fire department to show up. When I told them that the fire department was right across the street from the police station, they said they hadn't realized it was that close. Before they thought of another plan, Hank gave us the word to come inside.

We sat in the kitchen eating cookies Mom had left out, and you could tell from the way Hank was smiling that Emily'd sounded great to him. Even Emily seemed up, and we had a pretty good time until Hank saw a couple of guys coming down the alley. He grabbed a bag of cans from the closet and told everybody he'd be right back. When he'd taken off with his cans and Emily'd seen what he was doing, she went over to wait for Hank at the back door.

When my brother came back up to the house a couple of minutes later and tried to open the door, Emily was pulling in on it.

"What's up?" he asked.

"Don't do that."

"It's the only way I can open the door," Hank said.

"I mean, don't give them cans."

"They're all right, Emily. They just don't have jobs or anything." Hank probably would've explained how the bums were mutes and all, but before he had a chance, Emily shouted, "Stop giving them cans!"

It was pretty weird when she did that, and even the Saltinis, who hadn't been paying much attention to what was going on at the back door, stopped swallowing cookies and turned to watch.

"I don't want them around," Emily said. She'd stopped yelling but was still plenty upset.

"They're not like you probably think. One of the guys just now told me his name was Arthur and he seemed real nice."

I was pretty shocked to hear that one of them had spoken, but Emily wasn't impressed: "I feel bad when I see them."

"They make me feel sad, too, Emily, but I think they're happier when I give them the cans."

"They're not happier. How could they be happier?"

I should've kept my mouth shut, but I hate it when people start letting everyone know how they really feel, and I think Emily was going to say that the bums didn't have a home or anybody to take care of them when they're sick and that a bag of cans wasn't going to change that. So before she could get started, I said, "Maybe those guys are just crazy for garbage."

I didn't expect Emily and Hank to think it was funny, but even the Saltinis gave me a look. And I guess the moment for Emily to open up had passed, because she went out the back door, just about flattening Hank on the way. Her leaving dampened everybody down, and the Saltinis didn't hang around long. That left just Hank and me in the kitchen, and when he started washing glasses as silently as you can do that, I split.

CHAPTER 19

From the outside the police station doesn't look like it'd have a big meeting room, but it does, and the place was packed with senior citizens and police families and a lot of people who'd probably been forced to attend as a punishment for some crime against tomatoes.

When I went backstage to see how Hank was doing, I saw Emily, and I just about fell over, because she was actually dressed like a normal kid. I'd heard that she'd been to a psychologist a couple of times who was trying to calm her down, and it looked like it was helping, so I walked over and asked her how she was doing.

"I don't have any feelings in my hands," she said.

"What?"

"My hands are numb."

"That's crazy," I said, and then wished I hadn't.

"I know," said Emily.

"I mean weird, not crazy."

"My doctor says I have to start facing things."

"Did he?" I was looking around for Hank because I felt uncomfortable standing there talking to Emily about what her shrink had to say.

"He said I run away from anything unpleasant. He's here tonight."

"Have you told him about your hands?"

"I haven't seen him. He's out in the audience."

"Should I go get him?"

"I don't think so."

"Isn't having numb hands going to slow down your playing?"

"Probably."

"Aren't you worried about that?"

"A lot."

"Maybe it'll pass."

"Maybe."

"Even if it doesn't, I wouldn't worry."

"Why not?"

"Because I had the same thing happen to me last year when I was elected to Homecoming Court and was going to have to go out in front of everybody with this girl who's a great dancer. I kept thinking I'd trample her to death, so Mom practiced with me for a week, and I ended up doing fine at the dance even though sometimes it felt like my feet were on their own.''

"Oh," Emily said.

"Do you get the point?"

"There's a point?"

"Sure there's a point. The point is that I'd practiced like mad the way you have with the piano, and when the time came, my feet took over and did what they were supposed to.''

"I don't play the piano with my feet."

"I know that, and my point doesn't have anything to do with feet." Actually, I was losing track of what the point did have to do with, so I didn't mind when Allie showed up.

I told her about Emily's hands, but Allie'd already heard and'd been out in the audience talking to her folks. They'd decided Emily should try to play, which she didn't look too thrilled about, and I figured her only hope was if the Saltinis went ahead and pulled the fire alarm.

While Allie did some massage stuff on Emily's hands, I went looking for Hank, who I found watching the Saltinis get loosened up. It was pretty obvious there was nothing numb about them except maybe their brains, which reminded me of Emily, and when I asked Hank if he knew about her hands, he said he did. He looked pretty worried, but he didn't say anything, so I wished him luck and went back out front.

I got myself a place to stand along the back wall just as Judge Talbot walked onto the stage.

"Good evening," she said. "I'd like to welcome everyone to tonight's program, with a special greeting going out to the seniors in the audience."

When Talbot said that, some older people clapped like mad and one called out something about power to the Gray Panthers, which I guess is a political group for older people. I thought it was just as well the seniors were getting their cheering over with right away, because there probably wasn't going to be much to holler about during the program. On the other hand, it was scary hearing that panther business, because I didn't think elderly radicals would be the best audience for Hank's jokes.

"Tonight is about mending fences," the judge said. "It is about bringing this community together from one end of the age spectrum to the other." I started getting weak in the knees thinking the judge was going to give another speech, but instead she went ahead and introduced the first act, which was four policemen dressed up like barbers.

For ten minutes they sang their heads off, and most of the audience loved them; in fact, a couple fools even called for an encore. The cops were back onstage in a second, and when they finally dragged themselves away, the judge came back out and introduced a cop who turned out to have a pretty neat voice, but he sang opera stuff, and the audience got restless, which wasn't good for Hank, because he was introduced next.

If Hank was worried about that, though, it didn't show, because halfway through his first joke he was cracking himself up. Unfortunately, he was the only one who thought anything funny was going on. The audience was so silent, I tried to fake a couple laughs, and so did Liz and Allie. But I was getting depressed for my brother, and I sounded more like I was stabbing myself than laughing.

It turned out, though, that halfway through the routine a few other people started to laugh, and pretty soon you couldn't hear the actual jokes, there were so many people roaring. Hank got a lot of applause when he finished.

The Saltinis were introduced next. I could tell they were nervous, because they ran onto the stage and started throwing crackers at each other before they'd gotten into position, so that nothing got caught. I thought the audience'd get upset at having to watch a food fight instead of a juggling act, but everybody figured they were seeing another comedy routine, and when the Saltinis ran out of crackers and took a bow, they got a big hand.

That got them fired up enough to get going on their human pyramid, which went pretty well until they all lifted their right hands and waved at the audience. It looked neat, except the Saltinis on the bottom of the pyramid couldn't keep from sliding around on crackers, and when the pyramid started seriously shaking, the guy on top stopped waving and looked down. Right then the bottom gave way and the pyramid collapsed.

The audience thought that was even funnier than the food fight, and they clapped the whole time the Saltinis were getting themselves untangled and checking for broken bones. I figured they'd give up on the board-balancing trick, but the cheering must've gotten to them again, because they hauled their bricks out, and three of them got the board set up while the other two went out and recruited watches—the only people who didn't slip their watches out of sight when they saw the two guys coming were Saltini relatives and the Boggses and my folks.

When everything was set up, Judge Talbot came out and blindfolded the Saltinis and got them onto the board. When she gave the word, they started wobbling along like they were going to fall any second. They'd added a lot of arm swinging to the routine since I'd seen it in the living room, and there was one guy who kept going backward and forward, acting like he was real confused. After a couple of minutes all five of them managed to make it to the middle of the board, and while they were fighting to get by each other, you could hear a loud creaking—I figured someone was playing a tape recorder off stage which I thought was a nice touch.

When the creaking got so loud the Saltinis could hear it over their struggling sounds, they stopped moving. The audience was eating the whole thing up, and when the five guys looked down in this real careful way, everybody roared. It got even funnier when one of the guys on the board started taking this real gentle step down toward the floor. But right when he did that, the creaking exploded into a giant crack. The watches that weren't smashed by the board were crushed by falling Saltinis.

There was a lot of confusion for a while with people coming up to claim bits of watch, and the cops checking to see which of the knots Hank had noticed the week before was the one that gave way.

I thought the whole thing was funny, but then, I'd left my watch at home, and that might've made a difference.

When everybody got reseated, there was a lot of muttering about the cost of having watches fixed, and people were trying to imitate the sound the board'd made when it snapped. The judge came out, and when she'd quieted down the audience a little, she introduced the last act.

If I hadn't known Emily, I would've thought her coming out was funny, because here was this kid walking through crackers no one had bothered to clean up and having to step over the broken board and watch straps that were still in the middle of the stage.

You could tell Emily was scared, and I didn't think there was a chance she'd ever get around to playing, but she poised her hands over the keys and started to move her fingers around. At first she was touching the piano so lightly, you couldn't hear anything, especially since the Saltini's relatives were still grumbling. But Emily kept going and everyone started to see that unless they shut up, the piano playing was going to be all movement and no sound. So it got quieter and I could hear enough of what Emily was playing to know she was doing something classical, which I figured would lose her the audience for sure. But I was wrong, because the noise kept dying away, and except for Emily's playing the place got still.

As she went along, I think Emily forgot there was anyone watching, because her hands seemed to blend into the keyboard, and the music started to flow out into the room—which sounds weird, and it's

not the sort of thing I explain very well, but sometimes a musican'll play something simply, like the
composer probably wanted it done. When people
hear music played like that, they appreciate it, and in
the police station that night no one coughed or
turned around to talk or did anything else distracting, and the music kept growing until it filled the
room. The end, when it came, was sudden. But the
final notes hung in the air.

At first everybody was quiet, and Emily sat staring down at the keyboard with what looked a lot like
a smile on her face. And when she finally stood up,
so did everyone else. We were clapping, and I was
whistling like mad. Even after Emily'd left the stage,
everybody kept cheering, which was crazy, considering all we'd heard was a kid playing some classical
piano. After a while we realized that and settled back
down, but not right away.

When we were seated the judge came out, and
after she'd thanked everyone for showing up, she
called the performers out one by one. They all got a
big hand, and that guy who'd yelled the Gray Panther thing kept calling "Bravo!" while Emily was taking her bows.

After it was all over, I went backstage and found
Hank standing around with a giant smile on his face.
When he saw me, he said "See!" a million times, and
I didn't ask what he meant, because Emily walked up

and Hank gave her a hug that must've cracked half her ribs; but she didn't complain.

I would've told her how much I'd liked her playing, but she'd been hanging around Hank so long, it probably wouldn't have mattered to her what anybody thought. So when Hank let her go, I just asked her how her hands felt. She said that they were still numb, and you're not going to believe this, but it's such a habit of mine to say "That's crazy" that I did. She just nodded her head, and I don't have a clue what she was thinking.

Allie and her parents showed up, and they were all breaking their faces smiling. Allie gave Hank a hug and me a smile she must've been saving up for, and I won't even tell you what that did to my breathing, because you've got to be tired hearing about that.

When all the Boggses had split, Hank turned to me and started saying "See!" over and over again, so I dragged him out front, where Dad was trying to put his watch back together.

CHAPTER 20

That Saturday was the first day of November and the first day in two months I didn't have to go to detention or work at the Boggses', so I would've slept late except my family was making a lot of noise drying its hair and blowing leaves around the backyard. I finally stuck my head under the covers, even though that's usually something I don't like to do because it'll make me dream I'm in a cave suffocating.

But that Saturday I dreamed I was on an operating table, and Susan Cabot was dressed up like a surgeon—which is funny, because she can't file her nails without closing her eyes. I guess Mom and Dad thought my heart wasn't working right, and they'd hired Cabot to fix it. Somehow she'd used Liz's hair dryer to get my chest opened up and was taking stuff out and holding it up to Dad and asking, "Is this it?"

Dad would use his leaf blower to blast away at the thing until it was dry enough to get a good look at, but then he'd never have an opinion as to what it was. So Cabot'd show the thing to Mom and ask, "Is this it?" again. All Mom'd say was what beautiful internal organs I had, which Cabot wasn't interested in. Finally she'd toss whatever she was holding to Allie, who'd smile at the liver or pancreas or whatever it was, and that'd make the thing turn into a flower, which made Cabot so mad she'd snatch the flower away and stuff it back inside my chest.

Nobody had bothered to knock me out, so I asked Cabot if she could find a pancreas or liver instead of flowers to put back in me. But she just looked down and in this deep man's voice I'd never heard her use before, said, "Thanks for the invitation."

I looked around to see if there was a real doctor in the operating room who could take over, but there wasn't. And when I looked back at Cabot, she said, in Hank's voice this time, "Don't forget that the party starts at two."

Some dreams you never want to end, but I wasn't having one of those. When I woke up, I heard conversation going on in the backyard that'd been getting into my dreams, which are weird enough without other people's words being in them. So instead of trying to get back to sleep, I got dressed and went downstairs to the kitchen.

Dad and Hank came in while I was having some breakfast, and Hank was excited to tell me about the guy named Arthur who he'd talked to once before in the alley but only for a minute. Today Hank and this guy Arthur'd had a big-deal conversation while Dad was blowing leaves around the backyard.

When I asked Dad if it was a good idea to let a ten-year-old talk with strangers, Dad said he'd gone right over as soon as he'd seen Arthur. According to Dad there wasn't anything suspicious about the guy; in fact, Arthur introduced himself in a regular way and the three of them'd had such a great conversation that Hank'd asked Dad if Arthur could come to the party we were having that afternoon. The party was a replacement for the barbecue that'd been raided.

I told both of them I thought they were crazy, and I guess my brother wasn't interested in listening to me right then, because he split. "Your brother doesn't ask many favors," Dad said when Hank had gone into the house.

"Thank God."

"This is important to him."

"So?"

"So we can do it."

"If he wanted to take a bag lady on vacation with us, would we do that too?"

"There's nothing wrong with Arthur coming to dinner."

"What was he doing when Hank met him?"

"Looking for aluminum, I suppose."

"In the garbage?"

"Yes."

"Can I hose him down before we let him in the house?"

"If you're not going to be serious about this, I'm not going to discuss it."

"I am being serious. The guy might have stuff stuck to him."

"Arthur uses a pole that has a nail in the end to keep himself clear of the trash."

"A pole?"

"That's right."

"Maybe he'll let Mom use it tonight to serve potatoes."

"That's not funny."

"Neither is you getting talked into inviting a bum to dinner."

"Nobody got talked into anything."

"I bet."

"Arthur didn't even want to come."

"Did you have to promise him a car battery?"

"Has anyone ever told you, Richard, that you have a narrow view of human worth?"

"You have, Dad, lots."

"Doesn't that bother you?"

"The only thing bothering me is that Arthur might bring friends along, and we won't have enough brown paper bags to serve drinks in."

"Arthur's not bringing any friends."

"That's what you say."

"He only agreed to come because he didn't want to hurt your brother's feelings, which is more than I can say for you."

I guess that was supposed to make me feel guilty, but it didn't; and I went up to Hank's room to let him know that if any of my friends found out about Arthur, I was going to drop out of school. But before I could mention that, Hank said, "You haven't even met him yet."

"I've smelled enough of those guys to know I don't want to share a dinner table with them."

"Arthur showers every day."

"It doesn't rain that often."

"He pays a dollar and uses the YMCA."

"Is that what he told you?"

"Yes."

"And you believed him?"

"He's very clean."

"For a bum."

"Don't call him that?"

"How about derelict?"

"Arthur calls himself a citizen of the street."

"What do you think Emily's going to call him?"

"What do you mean?"

"You know how she hates it when those guys are even in the alley. What'll she do when she finds out one of them is passing her the butter?"

"Emily's feeling a lot better lately."

"This should take care of that."

"I talked to Arthur about Emily, and he said we should just not tell her anything that might get her upset."

"Won't she get suspicious when Arthur grabs the first empty pop can he sees and tosses it into his bag?"

"He's not like that."

"That's right. I forgot about his pole. He's just going to sit there and stab at every piece of aluminum foil Mom takes off a dish."

You can go just so far with Hank before he clams up on you, and I guess I'd gotten there, because suddenly he had nothing to say. The two of us sat around without talking until Liz showed up, and when I filled her in on what was going on, she was surprised but not upset like she should've been. I mean, having a bum to dinner was going to seem just as crazy to her friends as it would be to mine. In fact, if Matt's family found out, Liz would have to get a divorce from our family before her boyfriend's sisters would allow her near their house again. But Liz just said that if the guy was okay with Hank, he was okay with her. I would've liked to have punched her for that, but I didn't.

CHAPTER 21

Arthur showed up at two, and I was surprised when I saw him, because his clothes were a little old-fashioned, but otherwise they were okay.

He was about ten years older than Dad, and he gave me a handshake when we were introduced, which usually I hate. But when he said he was pleased to meet me, he sounded like he meant it, and I stopped being mad about his being there. Emily shook hands with Arthur and smiled at him, and I was thinking that she was looking more normal than her sister—even though Allie just had jeans and a sweater on, she looked outstanding, and I told her that. She said I looked great, too, which probably wasn't a total lie, because I had on a new shirt I'd bought to wear that day. That blue one had ended up as a cleaning rag.

I was feeling pretty good, and I think everybody else was, too, because when Dad suggested we play touch football, the only two to beg off were Mom and Mrs. Boggs.

We split the teams up so that the Boggses and Arthur were on one side, and Liz, Hank, Dad, and I were on the other. Mom and Mrs. Boggs were supposed to cheer for their families, but that turned out to be a farce. Whenever somebody'd make a great play, instead of jumping around, the cheerleaders would squeeze their beer cans in and out and make a crazy ponking noise. It didn't sound like any cheering I'd ever heard, but it amused the hell out of them.

If you've never played touch football, it's not a game that takes a lifetime to learn. You just have one guy on a team be a passer while everybody else runs around yelling that they're open. The passer has to throw the ball as soon as he can because someone's guarding him that can rush in ten seconds after the ball's snapped. I was the passer for our team and Emily was for the Boggses. Usually the passer has to be older, but Mr. Boggs said that Emily had a great arm and he was right.

In fact, one time I was jumping up to block a pass and Emily drilled me right in the forehead with the ball. For a few seconds I saw ten Emilys. When they got back together, she said she was sorry, but I think she nailed me on purpose to make me stop jumping in front of her. It worked, because I was afraid I'd get brain damaged if she hit me like that again.

That didn't make her lighten up when it was her turn to rush me, though, because if I didn't get the ball off right away, she'd tackle me. And it didn't matter how many times I explained that we were only playing touch football. Once I'd faded all the way back to our pool-neighbor's fence and was drawing back my arm to throw the ball when Emily plowed into me. I guess I should've thought to dodge out of her way, but I didn't, and I flipped right over into the neighbor's yard—and got out of there fast.

When the cheerleaders saw I was up and okay, they started ponking their cans like mad for the play Emily'd made. I went over to Mom and explained how she was only supposed to be cheering when the team I was on did something good, and my getting knocked backward over a fence wasn't a great play for our side. Mom smiled and said how much she was enjoying the game and asked me to explain which team I was on, exactly.

As rough as Emily was being on me, the best action was between Allie and Liz, which was funny when you think about it. Normally Liz has no interest in sports, but she played Allie tough the whole game. It helped Liz that it was her backyard, because what she ended up doing was running toward a bush or a tree while she was looking back for the ball. Whenever Liz was looking for a pass like that, Allie had to turn around, too, and at the last second Liz'd angle away from whatever she knew was coming while Allie'd plow right into it, leaving Liz open for an easy catch.

You'd think Allie would've gotten upset about that, but she always laughed when she crawled out of the garage or someplace weird like that. I noticed, though, that the next time the Boggses had the ball, Allie made sure that at least once she put on some moves that left Liz spinning around.

Hank and Arthur were guarding each other, and at first I thought Arthur being so much bigger might be dangerous for Hank, but it never was. In fact, Hank wasn't any better than Emily at remembering we were only playing touch football. But even when Hank'd make a crushing tackle and they'd both fall and wrestle around on the ground, it was always Arthur who'd come up with the bruises and Hank with the ball. Whenever he'd realize how rough he was being, Hank would apologize, but then on the next play, he'd do the same thing.

The only two guys not really into the game were Dad and Mr. Boggs. They almost always ran their pass patterns over by the cheerleaders so they could get beer and kisses—which I thought was corny, but there wasn't much I could do about it.

Once I did throw over there to see if they were paying attention, and the ball hit Dad in the arm while he was taking a drink. Dad got covered with beer and he missed a couple plays while he went inside and changed his shirt. When he finally got back and into the huddle, he said there was to be no more throwing the ball toward the cheerleaders unless I was looking to get myself grounded for life.

I can't tell you what the final score was because it was one of those games where nobody keeps track. Personally, I get more excited if I know my team's just ahead or just behind, but when you get a bunch of guys like Hank and Emily who just want to make the perfect play, it's not worth trying to keep score. When I did, they all ended up arguing with me, and my own team accused me of cheating. I knew they were teasing, but it irritated me anyway, and I stopped keeping track of points, which gave me more time to concentrate on avoiding Emily's tackle.

It was a warm day for the first of November, but when trees started blocking off the sun, it got cool enough in the backyard that everybody decided the next team to score would be the winner. We flipped a bottle cap to see who'd get the ball first. The Boggses won and on the first play I went running in to try to block Emily's pass, but she threw a bullet that I barely got down out of the way of. It was so low, Arthur had to drop to his knees to catch it, and when Hank went plowing into him, the ball bounced into the air and toward Mom. She put her hands out and made the catch. When Mrs. Boggs saw that, she jumped up and down and yelled that the cheerleaders had won.

That pretty much ended the game, so Liz and Mom went into the kitchen to get dinner ready while everybody else waited in the living room for Liz's boyfriend to show up. He eats with us whenever he can, and he always asks if he can pick up a dessert or my aunt Odell.

Odell's my father's sister, and she comes over every couple of months, which I don't mind because she isn't boring like Dad. In fact, she's a little weird and won't own a car because automobiles are such polluters. That doesn't stop her, though, from accepting rides, and she was happy to get a lift from Matt.

The two of them showed up late, and instead of making introductions in the living room, Dad introduced his sister to the Boggses and Arthur while everybody was getting seated in the dining room. As the food was passed around, my aunt looked at me and said, "Which is it tonight?"

"Which is what?" I asked.

"Are you Clint or Richard?"

Two months before, when I'd embarrassed myself with that renaming business, Aunt Odell had told me I'd define myself with actions, not labels.

"I'm Richard," I said at the dinner table, and I tried to sound confused, like I couldn't remember what my aunt was talking about.

"Did I ever mention, Richard, that we are known by what we do, not what we're called?"

Instead of answering, I passed one of my hands across my throat, like I was having a mid-meal stretch, the way you would if you wanted to secretly signal your aunt to change subjects. After a second, Odell turned to Mom and said, "I'm sorry you had to wait dinner, Kate. I wasn't ready when Matt came to pick me up. I'd forgotten that your boss furloughed you from the graveyard shift tonight."

"My hours aren't *that* bad, Odell."

"Arranging employees' schedules is difficult," Dad said, and he looked around the table for someone to help him defend management from his sister.

"I'm my only employee," Mr. Boggs said. "And I don't give myself much trouble."

"But you can still appreciate the scheduling difficulties Mr. Gilbert must face."

"I don't know what running a store in the mall involves."

While Dad was giving Mr. Boggs a look like he

shouldn't ever bother applying for membership in the Chamber of Commerce, Aunt Odell asked Mrs. Boggs if she worked outside the home.

"Yes, I do."

"Does your boss always schedule you for night shifts?"

"The museum I work at has no evening hours."

My aunt looked at Mrs. Boggs for a moment and then said, "You work at the Gunther Museum, don't you?"

"Yes, I do," Mrs. Boggs said.

"We've met before."

"You came into the office last year to complain that the museum was hanging its paintings too high."

"Was I rude?"

"You were insistent."

"Have you lowered the paintings?"

"We didn't want it to look like we were letting you tell us our job, so we had the floors raised instead."

Everyone laughed at what I guess was a joke, and that broke apart the conversation about Mr. Gilbert.

I suppose to be polite, my aunt turned to Arthur and asked him what he did for a living.

I looked over at Hank, because I figured he wouldn't be too happy about that, and he wasn't. In fact, he choked on his milk, and some of it came out of his nose, which looked gross.

"I'm retired," Arthur said.

"From what?" Mr. Boggs asked. He wasn't being nosy, but his following up on Odell's question was really putting Arthur on the spot.

"I used to run a projector in a movie theater," Arthur said. I don't know if he was lying or not, but Hank believed him. My brother's crazy about movies, especially old ones that only get shown on TV about three in the morning.

"You ran a movie projector?" Hank asked.

"Before they were automated. It was a great job as far as I was concerned. If I liked the movie that was playing, I'd watch it over and over again. And if the movie was lousy, I'd sit back and read."

"What have you been doing since you retired?" Mr. Boggs asked, and you could tell Hank was hoping that Emily's dad would choke on a chunk of the cacciatore he was having seconds of.

Aunt Odell had been watching Hank and Arthur, and she must've noticed that they were pretty uncomfortable with the questions that were being asked, because even though she'd barely finished her meal, she stood up and interrupted Mr. Boggs's questioning to say she had to leave. "There's a museum having an opening tonight, and I promised myself I'd go and harass the curator."

Everybody was pretty tired from the football game, and not long after Odell and Matt'd left, the Boggses and Arthur took off too. I would've crashed on the couch, except Dad volunteered himself and Hank and me to do the dishes, and I didn't get out of the kitchen until the only thing left on the TV was the news.

I went upstairs and didn't mind it when Hank followed me into my room and told me how when he had enough money, he was going to buy a theater that he and Emily and Arthur'd make a living at. According to Hank, most of the time they'd show only old movies that nobody'd be interested in except the three of them, which'd be fine with Hank because a lot of people who go to movies think they're home watching their VCRs and can make dumb cracks right out loud.

I asked Hank how he planned to stay in business, and he said that sometimes they'd get a picture that was lousy but popular so they could pay their bills and give Arthur a chance to get some reading done.

Hank'd invited Arthur and Emily over the next day to watch movies on our VCR, and he was going to tell them then about his plans. I wasn't thrilled to hear Arthur was becoming a daily visitor—he was nice and all, but he was still a street guy. And I would've said something about that to Hank, except you could tell he really liked the guy.

Sunday I drove out to the mall and rented the movies Hank wanted. When I got back, Emily was at our house making popcorn and helping get everything ready for Arthur to show up, which he never did. Emily and Hank sat around, waiting, the whole afternoon. Finally I told them that I'd gotten an afternoon rate on the movies and had to get them back.

They came along to the mall, and on the way Hank kept looking down the alleys like he expected to see Arthur's body lying in one of them, as if getting flattened by a garbage truck was the only reason my brother could think of for somebody standing him up.

Hank was trying to be subtle, but Emily saw what he was doing and said, "He probably had to visit someone else."

"You mean Arthur?" Hank asked.

"Yes. He wouldn't work in the alleys today instead of coming to see us."

"You know about him?"

"I saw you talking to him while I was standing at the back door the day we practiced at your house for the police program."

"And you weren't bothered having him come to dinner last night?"

"No. Things don't scare me the way they used to."

"How come?" I said, and Emily and Hank both looked at me like there was some stuff you don't talk about, which I'm sure there is, but I never know what it is.

We rode along a couple of blocks without anybody speaking, and then Emily turned to Hank and said, "You make me feel safe."

"What?" Hank said, and he didn't sound too happy.

"Something happened once that wasn't my fault, but it made me feel like I couldn't keep bad stuff from happening."

I know Hank should've been the one doing the questioning, but he was just staring out the front window, so I asked Emily what'd made her change her mind.

"Hank. And the program where I played piano and my counselor at school and even you."

"What did I do?"

"You weren't as awful as everybody said you'd be."

"Your feeling safe," Hank said finally, "should come from you, not me."

Emily looked at him and smiled. And when she reached out and held his hand, I could see why Hank was worried, because Emily was holding on like my brother's hand was a life jacket that was keeping her afloat in deep water.

"Who said I'd be awful?" I asked.

But instead of answering me, Emily told Hank not to worry about Arthur: "He just had to do something else today." She said that like her meeting Hank had brought violence to a halt and even guys who lived on the streets would never have anything bad happen to them.

Hank looked at Emily and then past her to me and finally back out the side window at the alleys we were passing.

CHAPTER 22

On Monday I rode the bus so I'd have a chance to ask Allie out. On a date. I meant to get to it right away when I sat down with her, so I wouldn't get nervous. Instead I brought up Arthur's disappearance. Allie thought something had happened to him, but I said he'd probably just started feeling restless and moved on.

I don't know what made me such an expert on the homeless except I'd seen a movie once where three guys traveled across Canada in freight cars, and I practically told Allie the whole plot.

I probably never would've gotten around to talking about a date if Allie hadn't pretty much asked herself out for me. She said I should pick a night, which turned out to be tougher than you'd think. Allie already had a date for Saturday, and Friday I was going to a church function with a girl named Yvonne. Normally I don't go to stuff like that, but Yvonne was the type that looks like they get themselves laundered every half hour. Usually girls like that only go out with guys who are class presidents or in college already, so when she'd asked me to a party at her church, I'd said okay just for the experience. It wasn't like I was going to take Yvonne up to the Overlook, and I told Allie that. But she said Yvonne was going to be a lot more dangerous than her date Saturday night and she was right.

Friday night I kept having the feeling that Yvonne was standing too close to me; at first I thought the ceiling in the church basement being low made everything seem closer than it really was; but then, while we were standing next to her minister, Yvonne told me that she was getting hot and wanted to go for a ride. As far as I was concerned, she'd said that way too loud, and when I got the chance, I told her that. But she didn't cool down, and when I hauled her home, she wouldn't let me get away until I'd given her a kiss. I tried to keep it formal, like the kiss was just part of an awards ceremony, but I ended up getting a better taste than I wanted of the butter brickle ice cream Yvonne'd been eating all night.

Saturday morning I went into Hank's room to give him part of the credit for the way women were attacking me in church basements. He had a bad headache, though, and was so nauseated he had to run to the bathroom while I was trying to talk to him. I figured he needed to rest, so I went downstairs to the kitchen to tell Mom that Hank was sick, but she already knew.

"I should've made him get a shot this year," Mom said.

"He wouldn't have wanted it. He never gets sick with anything but the flu, and every year he figures he won't get it this time."

"Did you talk to him?"

"I wanted to, but he didn't look like he was in the mood when he ran by me on the way to the bathroom."

Mom served me some eggs and toast and sat down across from me at the kitchen table. "What were you going to talk to him about?" she asked.

"I was going to tell him I've been using those ideas he has that everything's got a right way to be done."

Mom smiled at me like she loved having both her sons be a little crazy, so I said, "I'm serious. I started noticing how in most classes there'll be one day where there's a great discussion and everybody's real productive and then the next day the same class will be brain dead. After a while I figured out that some days the teacher manages to get himself and everybody else into harmony with whatever is being covered and other days he doesn't. It's like there's a current running through everything and the trick is to tap into it and get yourself an edge."

"Did Hank tell you all this?"

"Some of it. And some of it I've found out just by paying attention. For example, a lot of times when I'm talking to somebody who thinks they're saying something funny, I'll realize I've got my face screwed up into a grin that's totally phony. So what I've started doing is catching myself whenever I'm up to something that isn't in tune with the way I really feel."

"And then what?"

"Then I stand there without laughing if somebody's telling a joke I don't like. Or if a group I'm in is bad-mouthing a friend of mine, I walk away without making up any excuses. I'm doing a bunch of other stuff that you'd think would make people mad, but instead I'm getting treated with a lot more respect at school. Even gals like that Yvonne I went out with last night are more interested in me than they ever were when I was always trying to impress them. It's like I've found a gimmick that'll do me a lot more good than Dad's theories about making lifelong commitments to selling paint at the lowest possible prices."

"Are you making fun of your father's ads for the store?"

"Absolutely."

"I'd just as soon you didn't," Mom said.

"But they're stupid. That's why people remember them. It's like he's this clown who lives for selling paint, so everyone'd better go down and buy from him or his bozo heart will be broken."

"You know there's nothing clownish about your father."

"I know that, but why can't he make a living doing something with a little dignity? Something important."

"There's nothing undignified about running a hardware store. And the way your father does it, he's got the right touch you were talking about a minute ago."

It was pretty clear Mom didn't understand that doing-stuff-right business, so I didn't bother arguing with her.

I had to get out of there anyway, because I had a dentist appointment at nine and the receptionist at the office we went to acted like anybody who was late for their appointment was going to get their work done without novocaine. I could understand her wanting people to be on time, especially on Saturday, when most dental places aren't even open, but once you got there, you waited around an hour before the dentist'd see you.

I actually told the receptionist that when I got to the office—it seemed like the right thing to do, but it ended up causing more trouble than it was worth, because I got put so far down the waiting list, the only person I was ahead of was the lady who comes around and vacuums at the end of the day.

I got home a little after noon, and Mom had me call the Boggses to tell them Hank was sick and wouldn't be coming over the way he'd planned. About a second after I'd hung up, Emily was at our door asking to see Hank. Mom told her that Hank was probably contagious with the flu, but Emily said that didn't matter because she'd already had her flu shot. Mom called Mrs. Boggs to make sure it was okay, and it was, so Emily spent the afternoon in Hank's room, even though he felt too lousy to talk much.

When it was time for dinner, I went up and told Emily she'd better go home. She said that Hank was very sick.

"He's got the flu. It's no big deal."

"It is a big deal."

"Look, I'm glad you kept him company, but he's going to be fine."

"No he's not."

Her disagreeing like that irritated me, so I went over to Hank and asked him if he was going to be okay. He woke up halfway and said he was. But that didn't satisfy Emily, and I practically had to drag her out of the room.

Liz was staying with a friend for the weekend, but Mom and Dad were going to be home Saturday night and I could've made plans to go out but I didn't. It seemed like a good idea to hang around in case Hank started to feel well enough to play cards or something, but when some guys came around who were headed for the dance Allie was going to be at, I decided to go with them. When I told Hank, he asked me to stay home. That was unusual for him, but I didn't figure it'd do any good for me to hang around and watch my brother be sick. While I was explaining to him that Mom and Dad'd be downstairs, he more or less fell asleep, so I split.

At the dance I didn't get to spy on Allie as much as I wanted, because some jerks from Vicar High School showed up. They wanted to fight, which none of the guys I was with would've backed away from except if you get into anything at a school dance, you get detention for life, so my buddies and I went outside to a car we had some beer stashed in.

Actually, getting caught drinking at my school gets you in worse trouble than fighting, and we took turns sitting on the roof of a car in the middle of the parking lot so that if a teacher came along, we'd have plenty of notice. That's something we'd done before, and usually it worked out well.

But that night one of the lookouts got so hammered, he fell off the car he was on and into a trash barrel. While he was passed out in the garbage, the gang from Vicar came along, and because there was no one to warn us, the beer didn't get put away. The Vicar guys tried to serve themselves, which ended up in shoving back and forth, and finally somebody got punched.

Things got going after that, and I paired off against a short guy who threw a jab that was so low, I could've just let the force of the blow get wasted against my arms, which I was already holding up. But the beer had fogged up my thinking, and when I saw the punch coming, I ducked. My nose got flattened, and when it bounced back out to its normal spot, blood started draining out. I had to pinch my nostrils to get things under control, and instead of giving me a chance to take care of the damage, the guy from Vicar lowered his head and charged. He must've been more drunk than I was, because when I stepped aside, he ran by me into the hood of a car. The guy dropped to the ground and stayed there until his buddies threw him into the back of a pickup. I don't think he was hurt, because while he was being driven off, he sat up for a minute, and except for looking confused about what'd happened, he seemed okay.

Once I'd gotten my nosebleed stopped, I went back into the gym and saw that Allie was standing by herself. I went over and asked where her date was.

"He went to the bathroom. What happened to your nose?"

"I don't know. All of a sudden it started to bleed."

I should've told Allie the truth, but a lot of girls don't like to hang around guys who fight at dances, so I just asked if it looked broken.

"I don't know what a broken nose looks like," she said.

"It probably looks crooked."

"Then it's not broken."

"It sure feels like it is."

"Maybe it's broken inside," said Allie.

"Maybe."

"How was your date last night?"

"Yvonne gets worked up when she has too much ice cream. How about you and your friend tonight?"

"He keeps wondering why you're staring at us."

"I'm not staring at you."

"He thinks you are."

I saw Allie's date coming out of the bathroom right then, so I said I'd better take off. Before I left, Allie asked about Hank.

"He's still sick," I said.
"Emily's pretty worried."
"Hank's got the flu, that's all."

When I got home, I looked into Hank's room. He was rolling around, but when I whispered his name, he didn't answer.

Sunday Emily showed up while we were still eating breakfast. Dad told her the flu always hit Hank hard and he needed a lot of rest, but that if she wanted to see him, she could come back at noon. When she came back, she had a thermometer with her, and you could tell that irritated Dad, because we were already keeping track of Hank's fever and it was what you'd expect with the flu.

All day Sunday Hank stayed the same, which worried Mom and Dad enough that they called our family doctor. He said the flu strain that was developing was especially hard on children, but that if Hank didn't improve by Monday, my folks could bring him into the office. The doctor told them not to worry, though, because the only real complication that could come out of the flu was pneumonia, and it was too early to start looking for that.

Mom felt relieved, but she was still thinking about canceling out on a dinner that was being put on by the store where she worked. It was a once-a-

year thing where awards were handed out to employees for stuff like best attendance record. Mom always
looks forward to going, but that afternoon I heard her
telling Dad she was going to cancel their reservations.

I asked my folks if they were worried because
it'd be me instead of Liz taking care of Hank. Mom
swore it wasn't, but I made them feel like they had to
go to prove it. I thought that'd guilt them into going
for sure, but it wasn't until five o'clock, when they'd
checked Hank again and saw he hadn't gotten any
worse, that they decided to go.

Before Dad left, he told me to make sure Emily
went home by eight, which I figured she'd give me a
hard time about. I never found out, though, because
at seven-thirty she hauled me up to Hank's room and
told me he had a high fever.

I didn't think she knew what she was talking
about, but I took his temperature anyway and it was
a hundred and one. That's not surprising for a guy
with the flu and I told Emily that, but she said I
should take Hank to the emergency room at the hospital.

"Are you serious?" I asked her.

"Do it before it's too late," she said.

"You're panicking, Emily. Emergency rooms
don't want kids who've got a little fever and are
throwing up."

"Where are your folks?" Emily asked, and it was pretty obvious she was going to call them.

"They're probably in the car on the way home right now," I said. "And they told me to make sure you were gone when they got here."

"I don't believe you." Emily was getting more worked up all the time, so I called Allie and asked her to come over.

But even her sister had trouble getting Emily out the door, and finally Allie asked me if she could go up and look at Hank to calm her sister down. I didn't mind Allie doing that until she came back downstairs and said that she didn't think Hank looked right either.

"Of course he doesn't look right—he's sick," I said.

"But it seems like more than that, Richard. I've never had a real sore neck with the flu."

"Who says he's got a sore neck?"

"Emily."

"She's just making stuff up so I'll take Hank to the hospital. Did you ask him about his neck?"

"He didn't answer me. You really think he's okay?"

"I know he is."

"When will your parents be home?"

"Any second. And they'll check him out, so do

me a favor and don't let Emily call over here all the time."

Allie promised to keep Emily off the phone, and when they'd taken off, I started feeling guilty for lying, but what did they expect when Emily treated me like some half-wit who couldn't take care of his brother.

My folks got home at eleven, and by then Hank's temperature was almost 102, so they decided that if it didn't break by morning, they'd take Hank to the doctor's office. They talked a little bit about taking him in to the hospital that night, which I couldn't believe, and I thought about suggesting they get in touch with Emily for her opinion, but they finally decided against doing anything right away. Mainly they were remembering how when all of us kids were younger, the pediatricians had said that a fever by itself wasn't significant; it was whether or not there were any other symptoms along with it. While Mom and Dad were talking, you'd think I would have remembered what Emily'd said about Hank's sore neck, but I didn't. I just went to bed.

At three in the morning the phone rang. The call woke me up, so I went down to the extension in the kitchen and listened in. It was Mr. Boggs calling, and when I got on the line, he was saying how Emily hadn't been able to sleep because she thought Hank was dying.

"Couldn't this have waited?" Dad asked.

"I wouldn't have called if I didn't think it was urgent," said Mr. Boggs.

"Are you going to call every time Emily can't sleep?"

"Haven't you heard of people who sense something before it happens?"

"No," Dad said, and I think he was about to hang up.

Emily must've been on an extension in the Boggses home and figuring the same as I was about what Dad was going to do, because she broke in and said, "Go look at him." Emily's voice sounded like one of those that comes from under the floor in a horror movie, and it scared me so bad, I ran upstairs to Hank's room. When I turned on the light, I saw that there was sweat all over my brother's face, and when I felt his forehead, it was so hot, I yelled for Mom. She showed up right away and stripped the covers off Hank because they were soaked, and so were his pajamas. When Mom'd gotten everything off that was wet, we saw a weird rash around Hank's hips. Seeing that made Mom so upset, she started shaking Hank but he wouldn't wake up, and when Dad came in and saw what was going on, he ran to call for an ambulance. Even though Mom and I were down the hall from the phone Dad was using, we could hear him yelling at the hospital guys to get over to our house right away, which they did, because it couldn't have been more than ten minutes before they had Hank loaded up.

The ambulance driver told Mom and Dad that they could ride along, but it was pretty clear they didn't want me in there. I was clinging to Hank quite a bit and getting in the way, so Mom asked me if I'd be all right to drive to the hospital so we'd have a car there. I said I would and asked if I should call Liz. Dad said there was no reason to wake her up because nothing was probably going to be done until morning. When they'd left, I called Liz anyway, because I knew Dad was wrong about not letting her know.

She told me to come and pick her up, and once I did I must've been driving crazy, because after we'd gone a block, Liz made me pull over and we switched seats so she could drive.

The trip to the hospital wasn't long, but it's really clear in my mind, and I can still remember how empty and quiet the streets were.

CHAPTER 23

 When Liz and I got to the hospital, Mom and Dad were in the emergency ward with a doctor who was in the middle of explaining that Hank had an infection in his brain called meningitis.

I didn't understand most of what he was saying, and I got impatient because he was talking like we were medical students. I finally interrupted and asked if Hank was going to be okay. Just so I'd know he didn't appreciate being cut off, the doctor gave me a look before starting in about the drugs they were going to use. I interrupted again to ask how long the drugs were going to take to work. The guy looked at my folks like he was hoping one of them would shut me up, but Mom repeated my question. The doctor said that Hank's infection was a lot farther along than any he'd seen, and that he wouldn't make predictions, which killed me because it made us sound like we wanted a weather report. Before I could tell him that, he said we'd have to wait where we were until Hank's room was ready. That's what we did for over an hour, which's a lot longer than you really want to be in an emergency ward.

Right after the doctor walked off, a cop brought in two guys who'd gotten into a fight—and the way they were cut up, they must've been using lawn mowers on each other. After that an ambulance pulled up with a lady on a stretcher who was eighty at least. I guess she'd taken a wrong turn on the way to the bathroom and ended up falling down a flight of stairs. At least that's what her husband kept telling us. I didn't really want to hear about his problems, and I was going to tell him that things were tough all over.

But Liz started asking the guy things about his wife, like what her hobbies were, and that got him quieted down. Not that it's ever going to be peaceful in an emergency ward, because when the staff's not hauling cut-up guys or old ladies around, they're standing at the front desk cracking jokes, which really bothered me—I know the staff can't take everything personally, but they don't have to act like they're working in a nightclub either. I mean, at least the hospital could hire people who are naturally depressed most of the time.

Dad had to go over to a desk and give a woman our insurance information, which I guess the hospital needs right away so nobody tries to sneak in and die without paying. When Dad was done, the woman mentioned that there'd been a number of meningitis cases the last few weeks but that Hank was the first outside the transient community.

That was exactly what she said— "the transient community," like it was a new subdivision the bums left every morning to go into town so they could infect my brother with meningitis, and then at five o'clock they got on the "transient community" bus to go home.

"How do you catch meningitis?" I asked the gal who'd been taking our insurance information.

"You should really speak to your doctor if you have any questions," she said.

"He only speaks Latin. Don't you know the answer?"

"What's the problem, Richard?" Dad said, and if he'd made the connection between Hank getting meningitis and us hauling Arthur around in the Welcome Wagon, he wasn't showing it. At least not the way I was, because I was plenty sore.

"I just thought that for the ten bucks apiece

we're going to be paying this place for aspirins, we could at least get some information."

I was violating the point of so many of Dad's lectures, he couldn't decide which one to do first—which gave the clerk the chance to say, "I'll tell you what I know, and that is that personal contact is necessary for the disease to be transmitted."

"Could it happen while you're playing football?"

"I suppose it's possible."

"But you don't know."

"No," the gal said, and I think she felt bad she couldn't help me, because she called a nurse over and told her what I wanted to know.

"Meningitis is a bacterium," the nurse said. "It's in your nose and your saliva. Usually it'd take more than getting tackled by somebody to transmit it, but it's possible that—"

"Have you admitted a guy named Arthur?" I asked the insurance gal.

"I can't tell you that," she said, and before I could find out why, Dad hauled me away and shoved me into a chair next to Mom.

"Sit there," he said to me.

"It was Arthur, Dad."

"What was Arthur?" Mom asked.

"Arthur passed the disease to Hank during that football game," I said.

Mom looked up at Dad and he said, "Probably. Not that it matters."

"It doesn't matter whose fault it was?" I asked, but Dad was too busy letting his eyes water up to answer me, and for the first time since he'd come into Hank's bedroom and then out again to call the ambulance, he looked worried—I know he'd been worried all along, but while he'd been taking care of things, he'd been okay. But with nothing to do except wait, Dad must've started thinking about how Hank had been sick for two days without anybody realizing how bad off he was.

"If it's anyone's fault," Dad said, "it's mine."

Mom started to say she'd been the one in contact with Hank the most, but Dad didn't listen. Instead he sat down and started to cry.

Mom wasn't as shocked as I was, so maybe she'd seen him cry before, but I hadn't, and it scared me. And after a minute of holding Dad in her arms, Mom broke down, too, so that the two constants in my life had suddenly become variables. The only one who wasn't coming apart besides me was Liz, and she was off trying to find out where Hank'd been taken to.

I was afraid she'd start to cry, too, when she came back, which to me would've been fatal for Hank. I know that's superstitious, but it was important to me that Liz be under control, and she was. In fact she'd found out that Hank was going to be on the fourth floor and that he wasn't going to be in isolation. I hadn't thought about him being cut off from us as a possibility, so I wasn't relieved the way Mom and Dad were, but knowing they'd be able to see Hank helped them get back under control, which I was pretty grateful for.

While we were riding up to the fourth floor, Liz said she'd been told that the kind of meningitis Hank had wasn't as contagious as some diseases and that it was easy to avoid getting it if you were careful about hygiene and sanitation. It didn't look like that, though, when we got to the room where Hank was, because the nurses that were hooking him up to machines had gloves and masks and gowns on.

At first we thought we'd be able to go in once they had Hank set up, but when they were done, a nurse told us that because Hank was in intensive care we were going to be restricted as to how much time we could spend with him and only two of us would be able to go into the room at a time.

"How often?" Liz asked.

"Fifteen minutes every hour," the nurse said.

"Starting now?"

"If you'd like. There's a lounge down the hall that you can use while you're waiting."

Getting in to see Hank settled my folks down, and Dad was back to being an in-charge kind of guy when he came out of the room. In fact he found a phone and called the Boggses to let them know what was happening. I went along with him when he made the call, and when Dad was done talking to Mr. Boggs, Allie and I got on the line. She wanted to know if I was okay and I told her I was, though if Dad hadn't been there, I would've added that the two pillars who'd brought me up were showing cracks.

"Is Emily there?" I asked Allie.

"She's in her room."

"If you want, I'll mention to her that she was right all along."

"Dad just went up to tell her about Hank," Allie said, and she didn't sound anxious to put her sister on the phone, which meant Emily was having a breakdown or that she just didn't want to talk to me.

Either way I didn't push it, and Allie said she'd let me go. I suppose she figured I had a bunch of hospital stuff to do, like read Hank's chart or confer with the nurses, but the family of a patient never does that stuff. What they do is sit and think. And we kept checking the time so we'd know when two of us could go in and watch Hank sleep. The first time I went in it was a shock to see close up all the equipment he was hooked up to. But then seeing that stuff got to be reassuring, like it knew what it was doing, and what it was doing was making Hank better.

But the next morning two doctors showed up who weren't encouraging. One of them said Hank hadn't started to respond to the drugs and that it might take a while before he did. He wasn't kidding about that, because four days went by without Hank's condition changing.

At first we all hung around the lounge area together so we'd be there if something happened. Dad told the guys at the store not to call him no matter what, and Mr. Gilbert phoned Mom to tell her to take as much time off as she needed. Liz let the school know she and I would be out indefinitely, but once all those arrangements had been made, everybody realized we couldn't hang around the hospital nonstop or we'd all end up paralyzed from sleeping in the waiting room furniture.

At the end of the second day, Mom figured out a system where we'd each do two six-hour stretches every twenty-four hours. She staggered the shifts so there was a change every three hours, and maybe having two people there all the time sounds like we were overreacting, but I think we all felt we'd let Hank down once and we weren't going to do it again.

I think even Liz felt that way, though she'd been out of the house when it'd all happened. In fact, it was her idea to overlap our shifts. She said doing that would make it easier for one person to leave the lounge to go to the bathroom or down to the cafeteria. But I think she really wanted to make sure none of us was ever alone—it was bad enough sitting around that lounge when your family was there, but it was the kind of thing nobody should have to do by himself.

In fact a lot of the time I couldn't stand being in the room even with my family, and I'd go out and walk around the hospital. One time I was going by a room when somebody called out for help. I could see that the light above the door was on, but the hospital staff was always so busy, you could burn out your bulb before anybody'd come. When I went into the room, there was no one there, but I could hear some sounds from the bathroom. I knocked and a guy called out for me to come in. I did and there was somebody sitting on the john who'd dropped his cane and couldn't get bent over to pick it up. I started to help him stand, but he bawled me out and said I should just give him the cane.

After I did that, I hung around until he'd gotten back in bed. He said I shouldn't tell anyone he'd been up because he wasn't supposed to be running around. I said that if they wanted him to stay in bed, maybe he should. He told me that anyone who couldn't get around might as well have themselves buried. I didn't agree, but I wasn't going to argue with somebody as spunky as he was.

The morning after that I went back to see the old

guy, but he wasn't there. A nurse told me he was being operated on, so I waited until later the next day to give him some time to recuperate. Then I stuck my head into his room. He looked okay, but when I said hello, he didn't answer. I asked him how his operation had gone, and he pointed at the sheet covering his bed. I looked but didn't get what he meant until I saw that only one of his legs was outlined by the sheet. Where the other leg was supposed to be, the sheet was lying flat against the bed.

I must've looked pretty upset when I figured out what'd happened, because the old guy said, "It scares me too."

I know I should've stayed around and made up a bunch of lies about all the friends I had who'd lost legs and were still playing football, but I didn't. Instead, I split, and if you'd seen that guy's face when he said he was scared, you'd understand why.

When Matt came over to the hospital every day after school, Allie'd catch a ride with him, and she and I would sit on the front steps and talk. I asked her once why Emily never came along and Allie said, "She hates hospitals."

"Everybody hates hospitals."

"Two years ago our grandfather had a stroke and spent a lot of time in one."

I didn't say anything right then because I wasn't feeling very sympathetic—I knew it was probably hard on Emily having a grandparent sick and all, but next to having a brother get meningitis, it didn't seem like a lot.

"We lived down the street from him her whole life," Allie said after a minute, "and Emily used to visit him every afternoon. Then when she started school he'd come and get her in the afternoon and they'd walk home together. One day he didn't show up, and Emily thought he'd overslept the nap he always took, but when she got to his house, he was lying on the kitchen floor. She kind of panicked and tried to get him to stand up and when she couldn't, she sat down next to him and cried. By the time Mom found them, Emily was hysterical."

"What about your grandfather?"

"There was a lot of damage from the stroke and he was in therapy for three months."

"And that's when Emily got to hate hospitals?"

"Whenever she wasn't in school, she insisted on being there with Grandpa when he did his work, and she saw a lot of people who were in rough shape and not getting better very fast."

"Did your grandpa improve?"

"Not at first. But gradually he started getting back the use of both legs and his left hand came around a little at the end."

"What did your parents think of Emily hanging around a hospital so much?"

"They worried about it and tried once to keep her visits limited to the weekends, but she begged them to let her go every day. She said she was helping Grandpa, and in a way she was, because when there wasn't any therapy going on, the two of them would sit on the hospital's balcony and Grandpa would tell Emily about when he was a kid."

"And she liked listening to that?"

"For her I think it was reassuring to hear about older stuff that was safe and predictable."

"Where's your grandfather now?"

"While he was in the hospital, he had another stroke."

"He died?"

"It was two years ago next month. And it wasn't until just lately that Emily started to come around and be able to handle stuff again."

For some reason that reminded me of the old guy with one leg, and more or less to change the subject, I told Allie about it. When I was finished, I could tell she didn't think I should've ditched out the way I had. She even asked me to go up to his room with her. I said no, but she wouldn't give in, and she said it was the sort of thing Hank would do. That made me mad, so I said that if she wanted to go visit one-legged guys that was fine, but that she should leave me out of it—and that's what she did.

HANK

The next day Hank was a little worse. In fact, Mom and Dad both stayed at the hospital without a break, and when Liz was making the two of us something to eat before going in for her shift, she seemed more worried than usual. So a little after she'd left for the hospital, I followed.

When I got up to the fourth floor there was no one in the lounge, and while I was walking down the hall, there were nurses going past me in the other direction who were pushing machines that looked like the stuff that'd been filling up Hank's room. I started thinking that maybe he'd gotten better and didn't need all that equipment, and I was going to ask one of the nurses what was up, but they acted like they didn't recognize me and looked the other way. When I got to Hank's room, the door was closed, so I knocked and Liz came out. Instead of saying anything, she fell against my chest and started to cry, and I suddenly felt sick to my stomach. When I looked past Liz into the room, I could see Mom crying and Dad staring down at the bed where a sheet was outlining my dead brother's body.

CHAPTER 24

I didn't go to the wake because I didn't want to get a picture stuck in my head of Hank lying in a coffin. It's impossible to forget something like that, and when I told Dad I'd go to the funeral but that'd be it, he was upset. Liz got him to leave me alone, and I can't tell you how she managed that, because I didn't care enough to ask her. Actually, I wasn't interested in anything for a while, and mostly I sat and stared at whatever was on TV. Even the afternoon of the funeral, when everybody in my family was answering the phone and going to the door to get the food people kept bringing over—like they thought Hank dying had made Mom forget how to cook—I just sat around.

It was probably just as well my family had door-
bells to answer and food to put away, because whenever they'd sit down with me in the living room and
I'd start to explain what was happening on the TV
they'd start crying. . . . I never wished I had a tele-
vision in my room as much as I did then.

The craziest thing was that they started thinking
I was weird. At least, Dad did. He figured I should've
been talking about Hank the way the rest of them
were, but to me there was no use reviewing his life
like we were going to take a test on it. I didn't bother
explaining that to anyone, though, because people
don't get it when you're dealing with something dif-
ferently than they are. They just think your heart
dropped out of the car, and you never went back to
get it. So I kept to myself as much as I could, and if
anybody bothered me, I bit their heads off.

For example, at the funeral I was in the back of
the church before things got going, and Arthur
showed up. I knew he would. Dad'd gotten a phone
call that morning, and after finding out who was calling, Dad'd dropped his voice low like the CIA wanted
to put an agent in the hardware store. I went upstairs
and got on the extension because I figured it was Arthur and it was. He told Dad he'd just gotten back
from the veterans hospital in Miles City. He said the
meningitis had really worn him out and it'd taken
him two weeks to recuperate. He said that ever since

he'd heard that morning about what'd happened, he'd been wishing it'd been him instead of Hank that'd died. I thought about breaking into the conversation to mention how that was the same thing I was wishing, but I didn't. I figured Arthur had another reason for calling and I wanted to hear it. After Dad'd said that there was no way to know for sure who'd infected Hank, Arthur asked if it'd be okay for him to come to the funeral and Dad said it would. When I heard that I was so shocked, I thought I was going to be like Emily's grandfather and be found lying on the floor after a stroke. I actually stood in the upstairs hall hoping whoever found me wouldn't be like Emily and try to stand me up. But I didn't have a stroke. I just got mad.

And when Arthur walked in the back of the church, I blocked his way. At first he was going to try to get around me, but then he saw my face and changed his mind, which was just as well, because if he hadn't gotten out of that church I would've broken his neck.

At the cemetery, everybody in my family ended up getting strung out into a line, and people started walking along and saying how sorry they felt, like we were having a second wake or something. That was bad enough, but then the Boggses came around and Emily was with them, which I couldn't believe—I figured after Hank's death she'd be back to wearing nineteenth-century clothes and spearing kids with hatpins and that she'd never come to something like a funeral. But she was there and dressed normally and headed my way.

What I should've done was stand there and let her tell me what an idiot I'd been when Hank was sick, but I didn't. What I did was take off across the cemetery.

Allie tried to catch up with me, but I started running. I'd been avoiding her since Hank had died, and after a while Allie must've gotten tired chasing me, and not just in the cemetery, because when I finally went back to school, she didn't try to talk to me.

I didn't really talk to anybody except Liz, which was surprising considering what our relationship had been like before. But Liz never brought up Hank, which I appreciated. Sometimes on our way to school Liz'd drive out into the country, and we'd ride by fields that were getting covered with snow; and if that doesn't sound like something you'd ever want to do, you've just never had your brother die on you.

Liz and I had to go see the vice-principal whenever we got to school late, and after about two weeks the guy must've gotten tired of me lying to him about how Liz's car was breaking down all the time, because he turned to Liz and asked if she owned the black '53 Chrysler he'd seen around.

"Yes," Liz said.

"That's a nice car."

"Thank you."

"Do you ever have any trouble with it?"

"Not yet."

"Could you get to school on time from now on?"

"Yes," Liz said, and we started doing our driving around after school.

One night when we didn't get back until after dinner, Dad met us at the front door. You could tell he was dying to give us the speech of his life, but Liz said, "Not now, Dad." He shut right up, which was just as well, because I think if he would've gotten going about how I should be adjusting, I would've decked him.

Dad isn't the kind of guy who usually puts up with people acting the way I was, but I didn't care. And I didn't care at school who I made mad. I even started going out of my way to mouth off to guys like Stratton, which meant I was getting into a fight almost every day. I'd figured out that when I was fighting, I didn't have to think crazy stuff like how Hank was never going to get to buy a '36 Plymouth or run a movie house or marry Emily.

The only thing I didn't like about fighting was how guys like Stratton are liable to murder you if you don't know what you're doing, so I always tried to start stuff in a place where a teacher was bound to show up, and sometimes the only good shot I'd get in would be when the teacher was pulling the guy I was fighting off me. Maybe punching somebody while he's being held doesn't seem fair to you, but I wasn't worried right then about being fair.

One day on the way home, Liz asked if I'd do her a favor and knock off the fighting at school. I said I would, because I didn't mind giving up my career as a punching bag. Liz didn't think to ask me to stop fighting altogether, which I was glad of because I'd started doing something around our neighborhood that I wouldn't have wanted to swear off of. It was no big deal. I was just keeping an eye on the alley, and when any bums came around, I'd go out and give them a hard time. Usually all I did was tell them to get going. If they didn't, I'd help them along. Most of those guys are in rough shape and not looking for a fight with a high school kid, so after a couple weeks the alley on our block was pretty much bum-free.

That might sound to you like I was losing my mind, but at the time it didn't seem that way to me. I thought I was just getting something out of the neighborhood that didn't belong. When Christmas vacation started, I had more time, so I started watching alleys besides my own, and one time I came up behind a guy who was standing at the gate to the

Boggses' backyard. Right when I was going to tell him to beat it, Emily came out the back door carrying a bag of cans. She stopped for a second when she saw me, but she started up again and when she reached the back gate, she handed the cans over.

I waited until the guy'd taken off and then said, "What do you think you're doing?"

"Giving the man some cans," Emily said.

"Doesn't that seem a little stupid, considering?"

"Considering what?"

"Considering you could be kidnapped or murdered by one of those guys."

"The gate's locked and someone always watches me from the house."

"And that makes you safe?"

"No."

"Then you're crazy."

"No, and I'm not stupid either. At least not like you."

"I'm stupid?"

"That's right. You're ruining your brother's memory for yourself by going around bothering people he tried to help, and if you do that long enough, you're going to forget what Hank was like."

"That's quite a speech for a nut like you," I said, and then immediately regretted it, because Emily turned away from me and walked back up toward her house.

I'd been thinking about how she'd said there was somebody watching, and I didn't want it to look like I'd verbally abused the child, so I jumped the fence and caught up with her as she reached the back porch.

"Okay, tell me. Why give cans to the bums?"

Instead of answering me right away, Emily sat down on the back porch steps, like explaining something to me was going to be tiring. And while she sat there I started remembering how she'd waited on those same steps last summer for someone to ask her for a drink of water. Thinking about that made me stop hating Emily for the first time since Hank'd died, and while I was wondering if I should mention that to her, she started to cry.

I think it'd been so long since she'd done that, she didn't know how, and instead of putting her head down or covering her face the way you're supposed to, she looked up at me. It was cold enough that a few of her tears froze to her cheeks, and just when I was going to mention how her face reminded me of a wall I'd seen once in an underground cave, she said, "Because they need them."

"What?"

"I give the cans to the men in the alley because it's what they need," Emily said, and the day must've been getting warmer, because the ice on her face started to melt.

"You don't think they're going to appreciate it, do you?"

"It doesn't matter if they appreciate it. It just matters that I should do it."

"You mean it's the right thing," I said, because you couldn't talk long about Hank without getting to that. Emily nodded and stood up, but she must've been lightheaded from water loss because she sat back down.

"Doing the right thing didn't do Hank much good, did it?" I asked her.

"It's not supposed to. That's not why you do it. It doesn't have anything to do with helping yourself," Emily said, and her crying picked up again just as Allie came out the back door.

I'd always heard about people being so startled, they jumped into the air, but I thought it was an exaggeration until Allie walked onto the back porch and up I went.

It wasn't a jump that I needed a net to come down from, but I think it was noticeable, because Emily stopped crying and stared at me.

"Are you all right?" Allie asked.

"I'm fine," I said. "I leap into the air sometimes to keep my feet from freezing."

"I meant Emily," Allie said. "But if you want to come into the house to warm up—"

"No, that's fine. I better get home," I said, and

then a crazy thing happened—Emily came over and gave me a hug. It wasn't a long-drawn-out thing that'd numb up your arms, but it was a hug. And when it was over she went inside.

I stood there for a minute not knowing exactly what to do, and Allie must've figured I needed a prompt to get me going toward home because she said, "Will you call me later?"

I nodded my head and Allie went inside, but I just stayed on the porch and looked around at the snow covering the grapevines and at the garage and at the little holes my tears were making in the snow at my feet.

After a while I realized that if any of the Boggses saw me icing up their porch, they'd come out and haul me inside, which I didn't want, so I headed home. You'd think the exertion of walking through the snow would've helped me stop crying, but it didn't, and when I got home, I told Mom I'd be in my room and didn't want to be disturbed.

When I wouldn't tell her what was wrong, she went and got Dad, who was home for lunch.

He came into my room and sat next to me on the bed. He didn't say anything, and for a little while we sat there while I tried to get my crying under control. Finally I asked him, "Why did you want Arthur to come to the funeral?"

"Because he's a person," Dad said.

"That's it?"

"That's it," Dad said, and then he smiled and added, "A unique person, tame as you and me."

At first I didn't get what he meant, but then I remembered, and I started to sob. Dad put his arms around me and held on until I was ready to lay back and fall asleep.

When I woke up, I felt emptied out and still, like the streets had looked the night Liz and I had driven to the emergency ward, but I didn't feel angry anymore.

After I'd had something to eat, I called the Boggses' house. Allie and I talked for an hour at least, and once Emily got on the line to apologize for calling me stupid, but I told her to forget it and that she'd been right, which was the truth.

CHAPTER 25

That was all six months ago. Liz grad-
uated in May and she's taking summer
courses now to get a head start at college, which doesn't seem as crazy to
me as it would've last year. Actually, I did okay myself the second semester and ended up on the honor
roll. They're probably going to find out it's a clerical
mistake, but until they do, my parents are happy.

I'm getting along better with Dad, and we actually talk about Hank sometimes. Mostly what we do
is mention how Hank used to like this or that, but
once I asked Dad if he ever felt cheated that Hank
died so young. Dad didn't say anything at first, but
then he started telling me about the mayfly. He explained how that insect hatched out in the morning

and died that night, or the next. Dad couldn't re-member for sure if it lived one day or two, but he didn't think that affected his point, which was that the quality of a life doesn't depend on its length. At least I think that was his point. I might've tried to find out for sure, except I was late for work.

I've got my job back at the city park. At first I think my boss was going to hire a lawyer to handle the lawsuits from the people I'd be running over with the lawn mower, but it turned out he didn't have to, because I'm more careful now. I have to be because Allie and I are dating and I need the paycheck, though most of the time we just play tennis or go to the beach or walk around. And usually Emily tags along, which doesn't bother me as much as you'd think.

One Sunday afternoon Emily showed up by her-self at my house and wanted to know if I'd take her to the cemetery.

"Right now?"

"Yes."

"Why?"

"I want to leave this on Hank's grave," Emily said, and she held out a bunch of grapes that still had leaves stuck to it.

"Why grapes?" I asked.

"Flowers would die."

"Grapes don't die?"

"Birds will eat them."

"They're pretty green for birds."

"I soaked them in sugar."

I took Emily to the cemetery, but the next Sunday when she showed up with more grapes, I was worried that the first bunch would be waiting for us, rotting. That would've been a depressing thing for Emily to see on Hank's grave, so once we got to the cemetery, I told Emily I'd heard a clanking under the car and that I was afraid the drive shaft was going out.

"Will you take a look?" I asked her.

"You want me to crawl under the car?"

"If you don't mind."

"I've still got my church dress on."

"I parked where there aren't any oil spots."

"I've got my grapes and everything."

"I'll hold them."

"Won't you know better than me what's wrong?"

"I don't fit under the car. Just do me a favor and take a look."

"What should I look for?"

"Something hanging down."

"Where?"

"It could be anywhere, so you'll want to check

things out pretty closely, but stay away from the exhaust pipe because that'll still be hot."

"Are you sure you want me to do this?"

"I wouldn't ask if it weren't important."

Emily finally handed over her grapes and crawled under the car. When she was out of sight, I headed for Hank's grave. The grapes were rotting like I thought they'd be, and I tossed them away and got back to the car as Emily was getting freed up from the transmission she'd gotten wedged under.

"I didn't see anything," she said while she was picking gravel out of her hair.

"Thanks for looking."

"Are we going to make it home?"

"Why wouldn't we?"

"What about the shaft part?"

"What shaft part?"

"The one I was looking for to see if it was broken."

"You didn't see anything, did you?"

"I couldn't get past that big black thing."

"That was the transmission. How did it look?"

"It looked fine, I guess."

"Then we'll make it home. The transmission's a lot more important than the drive shaft."

After that Emily always wore jeans on Sunday afternoons, though I wouldn't have tried to fool her with the drive shaft story more than once. Instead I ended up going to the cemetery every Saturday with Allie to clean up the grave.

Last Sunday Emily and I were standing over the grave when she asked me where I thought Hank was.

"He's right here," I said, pointing down at the ground.

"I mean the real Hank."

"I suppose he's in heaven," I told her.

"Allie says Hank's in our hearts, too, and that when we do something the way Hank would've liked, the part of him that's in us comes alive."

I didn't say anything and Emily must've figured she needed to explain because she said, "Do you think the birds eat the grapes?"

"The grapes are gone, aren't they?"

"But do you think it's the birds?"

"How else would they disappear?"

"Someone could come and take them away."

"You mean like the guys who work here?"

"I don't think they bother stuff that people leave."

"Arthur could be checking on things, or maybe a bunch of the alley guys come out together. We might even see some aluminum cans lying around next week."

"They're homeless, Richard, not litterbugs."

"Right. No cans," I said, and Emily looked at me like she knew it was me cleaning up the grave, but all she said was that it didn't really matter because it was the Hank part of whoever was doing it.

Before I could say anything back, Emily took off, and while I was following her to the car, I realized that we'd probably come to the cemetery together until I went away to college. After that I think Emily'll keep coming until she goes away to school, and even then she and I will probably end up meeting on holidays so we can litter Hank's grave with fruit.

While I was thinking that, I got a picture in my mind of what Emily'll look like when the two of us are going out to Hank's grave in seventy years—she'll probably have gone back to wearing floppy hats and crazy dresses, but being seen with her won't bother me, because the way a person looks doesn't matter. I'm not exactly sure yet what does, but I know it's not stuff like that.

About the Author

James Sauer has been teaching for twelve years. He is a graduate of the University of Wisconsin, where he majored in history.

James Sauer lives in Billings, Montana, with his wife and daughter.

Hank won the Seventh Annual Delacorte Press Prize for an Outstanding First Young Adult Novel.